KU-201-614

PUFFIN BOOKS

Steve Jackson's Sorcery!

The Seven Serpents

Your quest to recover the legendary Crown of Kings from the evil Archmage who stole it has led you to the awful wilderness of the Kakhabad Baklands. Beyond lies your goal – the dark Mampang Fortress, where the Archmage sits plotting the downfall of the neighbouring kingdoms. If only you can reach it in time!

But your courageous mission is already in great danger! Seven deadly and magical serpents speed ahead of you to warn the Archmage of your coming. Will you be able to catch them before they reach him?

Steve Jackson, co-founder of the highly successful Games Workshop and author of many Fighting Fantasy Gamebooks, has created this thrilling epic adventure of sword and sorcery for you, with an elaborate combat system, a dazzling array of spells to use and a score sheet to record your gains and losses. All *you* need is two dice, a pencil and an eraser.

Many dangers lie ahead and success is by no means certain. Powerful adversaries are ranged against you and often your only choice is to kill or be killed!

The Seven Serpents is the third book in the *Sorcery!* epic.

THE
SEVEN
SERPENTS

PUFFIN BOOKS

Puffin Books, Penguin Books Ltd, Harmondsworth, Middlesex, England
Viking Penguin Inc., 40 West 23rd Street, New York, New York 10010, U.S.A.
Penguin Books Australia Ltd, Ringwood, Victoria, Australia
Penguin Books Canada Ltd, 2801 John Street, Markham, Ontario, Canada L3R 1B4
Penguin Books (N.Z.) Ltd, 182–190 Wairau Road, Auckland 10, New Zealand

First published 1984
Reprinted 1984 (twice), 1985 (twice)

Copyright © Steve Jackson, 1984
Illustrations copyright © John Blanche, 1984
All rights reserved

Printed and bound in Great Britain by
Cox & Wyman Ltd, Reading
Filmset in Palatino by Rowland Phototypesetting Ltd,
Bury St Edmunds, Suffolk

To Margery, Harry . . . their own special creation!

Except in the United States of America,
this book is sold subject to the condition
that it shall not, by way of trade or otherwise,
be lent, re-sold, hired out, or otherwise circulated
without the publisher's prior consent in any form of
binding or cover other than that in which it is
published and without a similar condition
including this condition being imposed
on the subsequent purchaser

CONTENTS

INTRODUCTION

The Seven Serpents is the third adventure in the *Sorcery!* series, following *The Shamutanti Hills* and *Kharé – Cityport of Traps*. But *Sorcery!* has been designed so that each adventure is playable in its own right, whether or not readers have been through the previous ones.

If you are new to *Sorcery!* you may prefer to start your adventure from the very beginning. The first adventure, *The Shamutanti Hills*, takes you from Analand, your homeland, out into the wilderness of Kakhabad, armed with a knowledge of magic to see you through your journey.

The Seven Serpents is, however, a complete adventure in itself. Set in the Baklands, a no man's land between the Cityport and the Fortress at Mampang, you must seek out and destroy the Seven Serpents. For these Serpents are the Archmage of Mampang's own messengers and they carry news of your mission back to him. But above all, you must survive!

New players will find all they need to undertake the journey as warriors. But if you would prefer the magic arts to the power of the sword, you will also need *The Sorcery! Spell Book* (reprinted at the end of this adventure) to learn your magic spells before you embark. Readers who are now on the third stage of their journey will be able to skip over the rules section and plunge straight into the adventure. Their characters, equipment and experience must be carried over from the previous adventure.

THE SIMPLE AND ADVANCED GAMES

Beginners may wish to start with the simple game, ignoring the use of magic. Rules for fighting creatures with swords and other weapons are given in each adventure book, using a combat system similar to that used in Puffin's *The Warlock of Firetop Mountain*, the original Fighting Fantasy Gamebook. By rolling dice, you battle creatures with weapons only.

More experienced players will wish to progress quickly on to the advanced game, in which your fighting ability is somewhat limited but your most powerful weapon will be your knowledge of magic, a much more powerful tool. In actual fact, the advanced game is fairly simple to learn. There is no reason why beginners should not proceed with the use of magic from the start. But learning spells will take some time and practice with the Spell Book (pages 199–218), and the 'simple' option is given for players who wish to start their adventure with minimum delay.

HOW TO FIGHT THE CREATURES OF KAKHABAD

Before setting off on your journey, you must first build up your own personality profile. On pages 18 and 19 you will find an *Adventure Sheet*. This is a sort of 'current status report' which will help you keep track of your adventure. Your own SKILL, STAMINA and LUCK scores will be recorded here, and also the equipment, artefacts and treasures you will find on your journey. Since the details will change constantly, you are advised to take photocopies of the blank *Adventure Sheet* to use in future adventures, or write in pencil so that the previous adventure can be erased when you start another.

Skill, Stamina and Luck

Roll one die. If you are playing as a *warrior* (the simple game), add 6 to this number and enter the total in the SKILL box on your *Adventure Sheet*. If you are playing as a *wizard* (the advanced game), add only 4 to this number and enter the total. Wizards are worse fighters than warriors, but they more than make up for this by the use of magic spells.

Roll both dice. Add 12 to the number rolled and enter this total in the STAMINA box.

There is also a LUCK box. Roll one die, add 6 to this number and enter this total in the LUCK box.

For reasons that will be explained below, SKILL, STAMINA and LUCK scores change constantly during an adventure. You must keep an accurate record of these scores and for this reason you are advised either to write small in the boxes or to keep an eraser handy. But never rub out your *Initial* scores. Although you may be awarded additional SKILL, STAMINA and LUCK points, these totals may never exceed your *Initial* scores, except on very rare occasions, when you will be instructed on a particular page.

Your SKILL score reflects your swordsmanship and general fighting expertise; the higher the better. Your STAMINA score reflects your general constitution, your will to survive, your determination and overall fitness; the higher your STAMINA score, the longer you will be able to survive. Your LUCK score indicates how naturally lucky a person you are. Luck – and magic – are facts of life in the fantasy world you are about to explore.

Battles

You will often come across pages in the book which instruct you to fight a creature of some sort. An option to flee may be given, but if not – or if you choose to attack the creature anyway – you must resolve the battle as described below.

First record the creature's SKILL and STAMINA scores in the first vacant Monster Encounter Box on your *Adventure Sheet*. The scores for each creature are given in the book each time you have an encounter. The sequence of combat is then:

1. Roll the two dice once for the creature. Add its SKILL score. This total is the creature's Attack Strength.
2. Roll the two dice once for yourself. Add the number rolled to your current SKILL score. This total is your Attack Strength.
3. If your Attack Strength is higher than that of the creature, you have wounded it. Proceed to step 4. If the creature's Attack Strength is higher than yours, it has wounded you. Proceed to step 5. If both Attack Strength totals are the same, you have avoided each other's blows – start the next Attack Round from step 1 above.
4. You have wounded the creature, so subtract 2 points from its STAMINA score. You may use your LUCK here to do additional damage (see over).
5. The creature has wounded you, so subtract 2 points from your STAMINA score. Again, you may use LUCK at this stage (see over).
6. Make the appropriate adjustments to either the creature's or your own STAMINA score (and your LUCK score if you used LUCK – see over).
7. Begin the next Attack Round (repeat steps 1–6). This sequence continues until the STAMINA score of either you or the creature you are fighting has been reduced to zero (death).

Fighting More Than One Creature

If you come across more than one creature in a particular encounter, the instructions on that page will tell you how to handle the battle. Sometimes you will treat them as a single monster; sometimes you will fight each one in turn.

Luck

At various times during your adventure, either in battles or when you come across situations in which you could be either lucky or unlucky (details of these are given on the pages themselves), you may call on your LUCK to make the outcome more favourable. But beware! Using LUCK is a risky business and if you are *un*lucky, the results could be disastrous.

The procedure for using your LUCK is as follows: roll two dice. If the number rolled is *equal to or less than* your current LUCK score, you have been *Lucky* and the result will go in your favour. If the number rolled is *higher* than your current LUCK score, you have been *Unlucky* and you will be penalized.

This procedure is known as *Testing your Luck*. Each time you *Test your Luck*, you must subtract one point from your current LUCK score. Thus you will soon realize that the more you rely on your LUCK, the more risky this will become.

Using Luck in Battles

On certain pages of the book you will be told to *Test your Luck* and will be told the consequences of your being *Lucky* or *Unlucky*. However, in battles you always have the *option* of using your LUCK either to inflict a more serious wound on a creature you have just wounded, or to minimize the effects of a wound the creature has just inflicted on you.

If you have just wounded the creature, you may *Test your Luck* as described above. If you are *Lucky*, you have inflicted a severe wound and may subtract an *extra* 2 points from the creature's STAMINA score. However, if you are *Unlucky*, the wound was a mere graze and you must restore 1 point to the creature's STAMINA (i.e. instead of scoring the normal 2 points of damage, you have now scored only 1).

If the creature has just wounded you, you may *Test your Luck* to try to minimize the wound. If you are *Lucky*, you have managed to avoid the full damage of the blow. Restore 1 point of STAMINA (i.e. instead of doing 2 points of damage it has done only 1). If you are *Unlucky*, you have taken a more serious blow. Subtract 1 *extra* STAMINA point.

Remember that you must subtract 1 point from your own LUCK score each time you *Test your Luck*.

Restoring Skill, Stamina and Luck

Skill

Your SKILL score will not change much during your adventure. Occasionally, you may be given instructions to increase or decrease your SKILL score. A Magic Weapon may increase your SKILL, but remember that only one weapon can be used at a time! You cannot claim 2 SKILL bonuses for carrying two Magic Swords. Your SKILL score can never exceed its *Initial* value unless specifically instructed.

Stamina and Provisions

Your STAMINA score will change a lot during your adventure as you fight monsters and undertake arduous tasks. As you near your goal, your STAMINA level may be dangerously low and battles may be particularly risky, so be careful!

If *The Seven Serpents* is your first adventure, you start with enough Provisions for two meals. If you have played the previous adventures of the series, the amount of Provisions you carry will already have been decided. You may rest and eat only when allowed by the instructions, and you may eat only one meal at a time. When you eat a meal, add points to your STAMINA score as instructed. Remember that you have a long way to go, so manage your Provisions wisely!

Remember also that your STAMINA score may never exceed its *Initial* value unless specifically instructed.

Luck

Additions to your LUCK score are awarded through the adventure when you have been particularly lucky. Details are given whenever this occurs. Remember that, as with SKILL and STAMINA, your LUCK score may never exceed its *Initial* value unless specifically instructed.

SKILL, STAMINA and LUCK scores can be restored to their *Initial* values by calling on your goddess (see later).

ALTERNATIVE DICE

If you do not have a pair of dice handy, dice rolls are printed throughout the book at the bottom of the pages. Flicking rapidly through the book and stopping on a page will give you a random dice roll. If you need to 'roll' only one die, read only the first printed die; if two, total the two dice symbols.

WIZARDS:
HOW TO USE MAGIC

If you have chosen to become a wizard you will have the option, throughout the adventure, of using magic spells. All the spells known to the sorcerers of Analand are listed in *The Sorcery! Spell Book*, which has been reprinted at the end of this book, and you will need to study this before you set off on your adventure.

All spells are coded with a three-letter code and you must learn and practise your spells until you are able to identify a reasonable number of them from their codes. Casting a spell drains your STAMINA and each has a cost, in STAMINA points, for its use. Recommended basic spells will get you started quickly, but are very uneconomical; an experienced wizard will use these only if faced with choices of unknown spells or if he/she has not found the artefact required for a less costly spell.

Full rules for using spells are given in the Spell Book.

DON'T FORGET! You may not refer to the Spell Book once you have started your adventure.

LIBRA –
THE GODDESS OF JUSTICE

During your adventure you will be watched over by your own goddess, Libra. If the going gets tough, you may call on her for aid. *But she will only help you once in each adventure*. Once you have called on her help in the Baklands, she will not listen to you again until you reach the Mampang Fortress.

There are three ways in which she may help you:

Revitalization: You may call on her at any time to restore your SKILL, STAMINA and LUCK scores to their *Initial* values. This is not given as an option in the text; you may do this if and when you wish, but only once in each adventure.

Escape: Occasionally, when you are in danger, the text will offer you the option of calling on Libra to help you.

Removal of Curses and Diseases: She will remove any curses or diseases you may pick up on your adventure. This is not given as an option in the text; you may do this if and when you wish, but only once in each adventure.

EQUIPMENT
AND PROVISIONS

You start your adventure with the bare necessities of life. You have a sword as your weapon, and a backpack to hold your equipment, treasures, artefacts and Provisions. You cannot take your Spell Book with you, as the sorcerers of Analand cannot risk its falling into the wrong hands in Kakhabad – so you may not refer to this book at all once you have started your journey.

If you have not played either of the previous adventures, you have a pouch around your waist containing 20 Gold Pieces, the universal currency of all the known lands. If this is the second or third stage of your journey, your quota of Gold Pieces will already have been decided. You will need money for food, shelter, purchases and bribery throughout your adventure, and 20 Gold Pieces will not go far. You will find it necessary to collect more gold as you progress on your way.

You are also carrying Provisions (food and drink). As you will find, food is an important commodity and you will have to be careful how you use it. Make sure you do not waste food: you cannot afford to run out of Provisions.

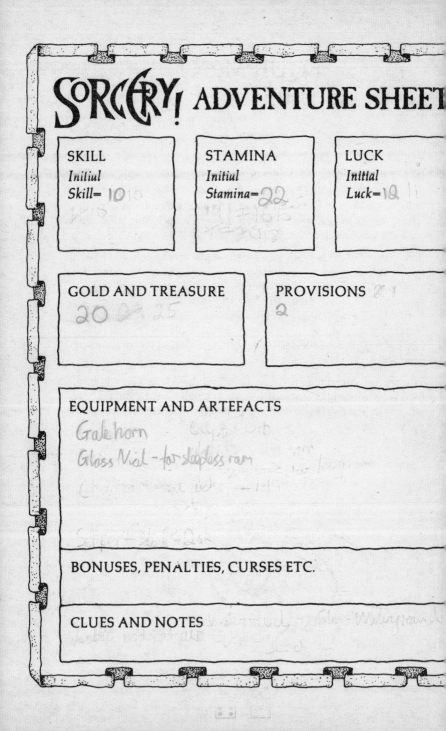

SORCERY! ADVENTURE SHEET

SKILL	STAMINA	LUCK
Initiul	*Initiul*	*Initial*
Skill = 10	*Stamina* = 22	*Luck* = 12

GOLD AND TREASURE
20 25

PROVISIONS
2

EQUIPMENT AND ARTEFACTS
Gate horn
Glass Vial - for sleepless ram

BONUSES, PENALTIES, CURSES ETC.

CLUES AND NOTES

MONSTER ENCOUNTER BOXES

Skill=
Stamina=

Skill=
Stamina=

Skill=
Stamina=

Skill=
Stamina=

Skill=
Stamina=

Skill=
Stamina=

Skill=
Stamina=

Skill=
Stamina=

Skill=
Stamina=

Skill=
Stamina=

Skill=
Stamina=

Skill=
Stamina=

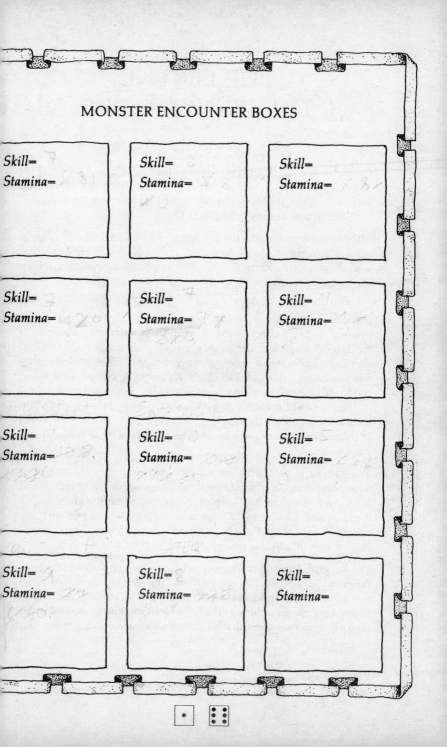

THE LEGEND
OF THE CROWN OF KINGS

Centuries ago, in the time we now call the Dark Ages, whole regions of the world were undiscovered. There were pockets of civilization, each with their own races and cultures. One such region was Kakhabad, a dark land at the end of the earth.

Although several warlords had tried, Kakhabad had never been ruled. All manner of evil creatures, forced from the more civilized lands beyond the Zanzunu Peaks, had gradually crawled into Kakhabad, which became known as the Verminpit at Earth End.

Civilization and order had spread throughout the rest of the known world ever since the discovery of the Crown of Kings by Chalanna the Reformer, of Femphrey. With its help, Chalanna became Emperor of the largest empire in the eastern world. This magical Crown had mysterious powers, bestowing supernormal qualities of leadership and justice on its owner. But Chalanna's own ambitions were not of conquest. He wished instead to establish peaceful nation-states, aligned to Femphrey. Thus in his wisdom he passed the fabled Crown from ruler to ruler in the neighbouring kingdoms, and, with the help of its magical powers, one by one these lands became peaceful and prosperous.

The path was set. Each ruler would own the Crown of Kings for a four-year period in which to establish order within his kingdom and fall in with the growing Femphrey Alliance. So far the kingdoms of Ruddlestone, Lendleland, Gallantaria and Brice had taken their turns under the rule of the Crown. The benefits were immediate. War and strife were virtually unknown.

The King of Analand duly received the Crown of Kings amid great ceremony, and, from that day onwards, the development of Analand was ensured. No one quite knew how the Crown of Kings could have such an enormous uplifting effect on a whole nation. Some said it was divinely inspired; some that its power was merely in the mind. But one thing was certain – its effects were unquestionable. All was well in Analand, until the night of the Black Moon.

The King was the first to discover that the Crown was missing. Carried off on that starless night by Birdmen from Xamen, the Crown was on its way to Mampang in the outlaw territories of Kakhabad. News came from the Baklands that the Crown was being carried to the Archmage of Mampang whose ambitions were to make Kakhabad his kingdom.

Although Kakhabad was a dangerous land, it was in itself little threat to the surrounding kingdoms. The lack of rule meant it had no army and its own internal struggles kept it permanently preoccupied. But with the Crown of Kings to establish rule, Kakhabad could potentially be a deadly enemy to all members of the Femphrey Alliance.

Such was the shame that fell on Analand for the loss of the Crown that all benefits from two years under its rule soon disappeared. Law, order and morale were breaking down. The King was losing the confidence of his subjects. Neighbouring territories were looking suspiciously across their borders. There were even whisperings of invasion.

One hope remained. Someone – for a military force would never survive the journey – must travel to Mampang and rescue the Crown of Kings. Only on its safe return would the dreadful curse be lifted from Analand. You have volunteered yourself for this quest and your mission is clear. You must cross Kakhabad to the Mampang Fortress and find the Crown!

1

The dark storm clouds roll across the sky as you start your journey across the Baklands. This stage of your trip will be the most testing yet.

The Plains of Baddu-Bak are unknown to the map-makers of Analand. Although certainly uncivilized, the Baklands are inhabited by nomadic tribes and solitary creatures. You will find few friends here.

But you must march on regardless. The crunch of your footsteps on the rough trail rudely interrupts the eerie silence hanging in the air. Apart from the great wall of the Cityport behind you, the landscape is featureless, devoid of vegetation, creatures or any structural punctuation to the horizon. An hour later, the barren waste has changed not at all. But in the distance behind you, the faint callings of birds can be heard. The noise gets louder and you stop. They are gaining quickly on you.

A sudden thought makes you freeze. Xamen Birdmen? Surely not this far from their homelands. Crows? No: crows' calls are not as piercing as these shrieks. Then what? You turn to face your pursuers.

From nowhere a black shape drops from the sky! You duck just in time to avoid the sharp, outstretched talons of the attacking bird as it dives at your neck! You steady yourself and clutch your weapon. The bird has soared past you and up into the air to rejoin its group. Four dark NIGHTHAWKS now circle above you, ready to attack.

How will you deal with these creatures? You may draw your weapon (turn to **258**) or use your magic (turn to **178**).

2

The Horsemen gallop off to the north-east. A short while later, the leader stops and points out a group of carts and covered wagons, arranged in a circle, in the distance. 'We will take you to within walking distance of the caravan,' he says, 'but no further. For they are armed and wary of strangers.' At a trotting pace they take you to within a few hundred yards of the camp. You dismount and they leave. You may now approach the caravan. Turn to **137**.

3

'Very well, traveller, do not heed our advice,' warns the voice. 'We will leave you to continue your journey, but we spoke the truth. You will never survive the journey to Low Xamen without this help. But if such is your wish, so be it.' If you wish to reconsider and recite the chant, turn to **297**. If you will stand by your decision you may now leave the area (turn to **133**).

4

After a brief rest, you can continue your journey. You will have to leave the swamplands soon for you are now in the shadow of the Zanzunu Peaks. Turn to **393**.

5

You try to get her talking about the Serpents but you can detect a note of hesitancy in her replies. She seems to be a little nervous about this subject. Nevertheless, she is able to tell you of some of the Serpents' weaknesses. The Fire Serpent is extinguished by sand; the Sun Serpent cannot abide water and the Water Serpent cannot tolerate oil. This is all very interesting, but more than that you cannot discover. Eventually you prepare to leave. Turn to **324**.

6

You spring to the left to avoid another crack. As you do so, the snake digs in its fangs, causing you to wince in pain and land awkwardly on your ankle. Lose 2 STAMINA points. You had better rid yourself of this little pest. Turn to **263**.

7

You watch for a little while as he plays his pipe and the snakes respond to his music. After watching the remarkable show, you decide to question him. Will you ask him whether he has anything he might like to exchange for something in your pack (turn to **121**) or will you ask him whether he knows anything about the Seven Serpents (turn to **161**)?

8

Excitedly, you open the Spell Book. But to your horror, you find it is a Spell Book from Analand! Somehow it has fallen into the wrong hands and wound up in Kakhabad, and this could be very dangerous for Analand. Each country's own sorcery is one of its most closely guarded secrets. There is no other alternative. The book must be destroyed at the earliest opportunity. Trying hard to keep your composure so as not to give your discovery away, you close the book. As soon as you are able, you will destroy the book – but you may first look through it to brush up your own knowledge of the spells. (You may if you wish spend five minutes revising the *Sorcery! Spell Book*, printed at the end of this adventure. At no other time are you permitted to look through this book once you have embarked on your quest.) Turn to **86**.

9

The crashings and rumblings subside. You jump to the left and narrowly avoid another falling rock but soon all is still. The danger has been averted. You may now either investigate the trapdoor (turn to **180**) or leave this place (turn to **309**).

10

As the storm passes, you consider your likely routes. Will you continue north-west (turn to **73**) or head north towards the forest (turn to **283**)? You may rest here and eat Provisions if you wish. If you take a meal you may add 2 STAMINA points if this is your first meal of the day or 1 STAMINA point if you have already eaten.

11

Which direction will you continue in:

North-west – a long trek?	Turn to **47**
To the north-north-west?	Turn to **15**
North-east?	Turn to **73**

12

You carry on tramping across the plains, watching for signs of life. There are none. But a curious sound in the distance reaches your ears. It gets louder as you continue – a sort of distant screeching. But nowhere is there any likely source of the noise. You look about quizzically and gasp in horror as you see ahead a pair of disembodied eyes glaring at you! Their gaze is hypnotic, but you shake your head to break the spell. The screeching noise is now very close and as you blink your eyes, you can see its source. Ten yards ahead of you there is a disturbance in the air. A shimmering heat-haze is rising from a craggy boulder. As it rises, so does the pitch of the sound. Whatever it is has been distorting your view of the landscape ahead! Some way from the rock, the shimmering merges with the eyes and the shrill sound turns into a high-pitched mocking laugh, as if a coven of witches were jeering at you. You stare in fear.

As you watch, the shimmering rises above the eyes and a fearful shape forms. A dark-cowled creature with a skull-like head beckons you over with a single bony finger. Will you approach it as it wishes (turn to **104**), will you run for cover in the rocks (turn to **185**) or will you turn back and run from the scene as quickly as you can (turn to **174**)?

13

As the sun climbs into the sky, the walk through the woods is a pleasant trip. Strange trees and bushes line the path and every so often you catch glimpses of birds singing in the branches. There may be some useful gatherings along the way. You pass, and may take with you, any of the following (but for each thing that you take, you will have to leave behind one of your current possessions): five small pebbles; a handful of green, leathery leaves with six lobes; some sand; enough nuts and berries for two meals; stone dust; feathers from a yellow bird. When you have decided and made your adjustments, turn to **117**.

14

You reach for the flask and wait for the Serpent to attack. It circles in the air and dives down at you. You duck quickly and, as it flies overhead, you shake out the contents of the flask at the creature. You watch in amazement as the oil takes effect. Before the creature can even utter a sound, the oil has broken it up into harmless splashes of water, which now rain down on the lake! You have defeated the Water Serpent. Turn to **75**.

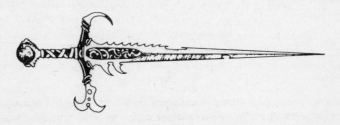

15

For a couple of hours you walk across the bleak steppes. A wind builds up and, to your consternation, it is blowing against you, making the going difficult. A boulder jutting out of the ground will give you some shelter if you wish to stop, rest, eat and wait for the wind to die down. Do you wish to stop here? If so, turn to **97**. If you would prefer to continue regardless, turn to **107**.

16

You settle down to sleep for the night. Add 3 STAMINA points for the rest and continue the next morning by turning to **230**. If you did not eat at all yesterday, you must deduct 3 STAMINA points.

17

Ideal travelling provisions, Vittles are small pastry balls with tough dried meat inside. You have bought enough for four meals. Turn to **86**.

18

You feel hot and prickly all over. The old Elf laughs at your discomfort. You are breaking out in red blotches all over your body! 'Don't worry,' he chuckles. 'This sometimes happens if you have not taken Whortle soup before. But the effects are merely temporary.' The other Elves are also laughing at your predicament. 'Cook!' he shouts. 'What say we give our friend a Gold Piece for the aggravation?' The cook agrees and hands you a Gold Piece. Turn to **231**.

19

As you near the village, you are noticed and several of the villagers gather together to watch you approach. They are ugly creatures, strong and lanky. They wear animal skins, and two tall males hold hefty wooden clubs. These KLATTAMEN are a primitive race, adapted to living a semi-nomadic life on the steppes. As you enter the village, they look at you with expressions which you cannot read. They could be in awe of you; but there is also a sly gleam in their eyes. They motion for you to follow them to a roasting fire, where an animal is cooking on a spit. Will you accept their hospitality (turn to **204**) or will you carry on walking through the village and on towards the forest (turn to **173**)?

20

You collect your things and leave the clearing. For several hours you follow the path through the woods. But you are aware that the forest is thinning. You must be nearing the edge, which means that you will soon be able to see the waters of Lake Ilklala. It is early evening when you eventually reach the shores of the great lake. You look out across the vast expanse of still water which stretches to the horizon and your heart sinks. How will you cross the lake? There are no signs of people or boats, as far as you can see. You sit down to consider the problem. You might as well camp here for the night and make your plans in the morning. You may eat Provisions if you wish. If you do, add 2 STAMINA points if this is your first meal today or 1 STAMINA point if you have already eaten. Then you can settle down to sleep. Turn to **264**.

21

As you bend down towards the old ferryman, the swirling Air Serpent becomes agitated and darts about quickly trying to fix itself around your face. Its choking gas will harm you if you breathe it in for any length of time. Poking through the ferryman's clothes, you find a shrivelled snakeskin and, as you pick it up, the Serpent rises into the air as if in terror. An unearthly voice cries out, ordering you to put the skin back. What will you do? Will you replace the skin on condition that the Serpent leaves you alone (turn to 131) or will you rip it apart (turn to 34)?

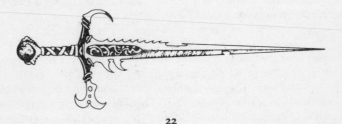

22

A smile spreads across the little creature's lips. 'Why, thank you for your gift,' it says. Its voice has changed to one which does not match its form at all, but is instead the voice of a woman in her middle years. 'Then it is true. You *are* of a lawful disposition. For none of Kakhabad would offer gifts to a complete stranger. But wait. Let me dispel this disguise.' Before your eyes she transforms herself from the small urchin into a tall woman dressed in purple robes. 'Allow me to introduce myself. I am Dintainta of the Steppes, although some call me The Sham. I know of your mission and I can help you. It is a credit to your wit and your courage that you have survived this far. But I warn you, much greater dangers lie ahead. At the Fortress of Mampang, 'beware the Sleepless Ram, for even your skill will be no match for its powers. You will overcome it by uncorking this vial in its presence.' She hands you a small glass vial. 'Guard this vial with your life and let no one release the gas within. One final word of advice. A short distance ahead you will confront the Earth Serpent. His powers are considerable, but these powers exist only when he is in contact with the earth. My thanks for your gift, and a safe journey.' Dintainta mumbles a few words and transforms herself back into her former self. With a wink at you, she sets off along her trail, while you turn back to yours. Turn to 114.

23

The well is old and dried up. To test it, you lower the bucket and pull it back up again. Hauling it over the side of the well, you peer inside – and spring back just in time to avoid being bitten by a golden snake which has coiled itself up inside! The bucket falls to the ground and the snake slithers out towards you. Will you draw your weapon to fight it (turn to **52**) or cast a spell?

ZAP	RAP	FOF	HOT	YAP
355	339	397	407	461

24

From the Beetle's hole in the ground, you may collect some stone dust. Then you must decide which way to continue. A long trek lies ahead of you. Will you head north-west (turn to **137**) or north-east (turn to **12**)?

25

You stop in your tracks. In the foliage to the left is a pair of eyes. A furry face is watching you. To the right, another dark furry creature is staring. You look around and freeze! You are surrounded by at least a dozen SNATTACATS! The two in front of you close their eyes . . . and disappear. Will you draw your weapon (turn to **74**) or will you cast a spell?

GOB	YAZ	GUM	FOF	FAR
358	398	451	383	423

26

'Of course,' says the old Elf. 'You must be tired after your journey, and night is fast approaching. Let me take you to an empty caravan where you can sleep for the night.' He leads you outside to a dirty trailer and hands you a blanket to wrap yourself in. Turn to **125**.

27

You manage to pull out your weapon. The position is awkward, but you can use it to cut your way free:

STRANGLEBUSH   SKILL 5   STAMINA 8

The Stranglebush will not actually injure you (its SKILL merely reflects its defensive capabilities), so if its Attack Strength is higher than yours, you will not deduct STAMINA points. However, if you do not defeat it within five Attack Rounds, turn to **305**. If you do defeat the plant, turn to **106**.

28

You take the boat carefully up to the disturbance to see what is happening. But you can see nothing. Perhaps this is simply a natural occurrence where an underground spring or air passage breaks through the bed of the lake. You shrug and sit down again, ready to take the oars. Suddenly, the boat lurches violently in the water! The bubbling has moved and is now directly under the boat! You are thrown from your seat and must *Test your Luck*. If you are *Lucky*, turn to **118**. If you are *Unlucky*, turn to **281**.

29

You reach down to pull out your weapon. As soon as your hand touches the shaft, a painful jolt passes right up your arm, causing you to pull away quickly. Lose 1 STAMINA point. You try without success to muffle a cry and the creature at the table turns slowly to face you. 'So!' cries out a squeaky voice. 'Fenestra has a visitor, eh? Who dares to venture unannounced into Fenestra's cave?' You introduce yourself, being careful to keep your mission a secret. Will you ask her:

For permission to leave?	Turn to **68**
For information about the forest?	Turn to **317**
What she knows about Lake Ilklala?	Turn to **252**

30

You cover your head and run downhill while the stones shower the ground all around you. Roll one die. This is the number of STAMINA points you lose as they fall on you. You may, if you wish, use your LUCK here. If you wish to *Test your Luck*, a *Lucky* roll will indicate that only the smaller stones fell on you and you may halve the STAMINA damage (round odd numbers up). The falling stones, however, roll under your feet, making it difficult to keep your balance. You slip, and land on the ground with a thump. Turn to **98**.

31

The bottle contains snake-bite antidote. It will immediately cure you of any snake venom you have been poisoned with. Turn to **86**.

32

As you draw out your weapon, the Deathwraith lets out a fearsome shriek and lunges at you. Resolve your battle with the creature:

DEATHWRAITH   SKILL 9   STAMINA 9

You will find that your weapon inflicts normal damage on the creature. When you have reduced its STAMINA to three or less, turn to **205**.

33

The little creature grunts at your offering. 'I have one of these already,' it declares. 'Well, thank you, anyway, for your gift. But now I must be going. Goodbye.' It shuffles past you and continues along the way you have come. What is your reaction? Will you shrug, bid it good-day and set off in the opposite direction (turn to **114**), shout after it and offer it something else (turn to **254**) or are you angry at its bad manners and would like to teach it a lesson (turn to **327**)?

34

Gripping the two ends of the snakeskin, you firmly snap them apart. A loud cry comes from the Serpent, which now hangs in the air separated into two parts. You rip up the halves until they remain as small flakes of skin. Above you, the Serpent has been similarly dispersed. All that remains are puffs of smoke which are soon scattered by the wind. You have found the Air Serpent's weakness! Turn to **213**.

35

The last Horseman begs for mercy. You say you will spare its life if it aids you in your quest. 'Noble stranger,' it pants, 'I know you seek out the Seven Serpents. My only offering is in this respect. My knowledge of these creatures is limited, but our race knows one clue to their downfall. One of them – the Moon Serpent – has a weakness. He cannot tolerate the power of the flame.' As you consider this advice, the Horseman seizes its opportunity and gallops off across the plains. You search the other two and find 4 Gold Pieces and a pouch containing fine brown sand. After resting for a few moments, you may continue. Turn to **273**.

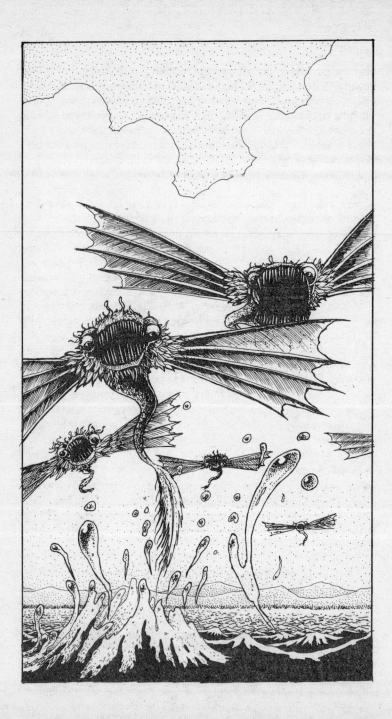

36

You take a wide detour around the bubbling water and then resume your course for the far shore of Lake Ilklala. A short distance ahead, another commotion in the water appears but this one is unavoidable. Leaping up from the water a small school of Flying Fish spring into the air and fly towards you. Although they are small creatures, their sharp teeth will rip your flesh and you must take defensive action. Will you cast a spell?

NIF	FIX	RAZ	WAL	PEP
403	373	360	426	449

Or will you fight them with your weapon (turn to 291)?

37

You explain your purpose and your quest for the Seven Serpents. At the mention of the Archmage's servants, a gasp comes up from the crowd. The old Elf holds up his hand for silence. 'So *you* are the reason why those evil creatures have come to the Baklands, spreading their terror!' He pauses to think for a minute, as if formulating a plan. Eventually he looks back at you, his eyes narrowing to slits. 'Well, perhaps we can help you, stranger. Follow me to this caravan over here. I think we might have something you will be interested in.' Will you follow him as he suggests (turn to 151), would you rather think about leaving this place (turn to 311) or would you like to cast a spell?

HOW	MAG	TEL	GOD	NAP
366	341	472	394	432

38

You are wasting your time trying to communicate with these creatures. Their language is little more than a series of grunts. One of the creatures picks up a stone and flings it at you, hitting your arm and causing 2 STAMINA points' worth of damage. You had better either draw your weapon (turn to 188) or cast a spell:

YOB	KID	GAK	KIN	GOD
475	439	456	344	356

39

'So the Analander has the Serpent Ring!' hisses the Serpent as it hangs in the air. 'Then I must tell you this. The Archmage is not as he seems. He may be disguised in Mampang. But then you will never survive to reach the Fortress!' Return to **53**.

40

You break through the chains and he climbs up the stairs slowly to accustom his eyes to the light. 'It's *wonderful*! And I thought I would never again see the daylight. Oh, how can I repay you? The Klatta-men took all my treasures. But you may have whatever's left.' You consider and decide that the most useful thing he is likely to be able to offer is his knowledge of the Baklands. 'The Seven Serpents,' he starts as you tell him of your mission. 'So they're about once more. Well, they are no friends of mine. I'll tell you what I know, but that is not much. You know already that they are the Archmage's servants. They are all vulnerable. But I know only two weaknesses. The Moon Serpent cannot abide fire, that is for certain. And the Earth Serpent is powerless when not in contact with the ground. But that is all I know, my friend. That is all.'

Eventually, after a short chat, you leave the old man and continue. But unknown to you, the cold and damp in his cell have taken their toll. He has the Yellow Plague and during your stay with him you have contracted the disease. Until you can find some way of curing yourself, you will lose 3 STAMINA points per day (deduct these at the end of each day). After the second day, you will realize you are ill, but before this time you may not take any measures to cure yourself as you will not have realized that you are diseased. Now leave the temple by turning to **309**.

41

You run quickly off down the path ahead. Invisible footsteps follow you, but eventually your pursuers give up their chase. You stop at a small clearing ahead to catch your breath. Turn to **20**.

42

Gripping your weapon between your teeth, you climb the tree. The red snake watches carefully. Suddenly, when you are not far from it, it drops out of the tree and lands on the ground below. You watch it drop and curse the beast. But your foolish move has left you at the mercy of the Fire Serpent. Once more the tree bursts into flames, but this time you are at the centre of the fire. Your clothes catch fire and you drop to the ground, screaming loudly. Lose 2 SKILL and 6 STAMINA points for your burns and the fall. At the foot of the tree you may now face the Serpent and attack:

FIRE SERPENT   SKILL 13   STAMINA 12

If you defeat the Serpent, turn to **306**.

43

Back on the surface, the danger is by no means subsiding. Cracks are appearing in the ground, radiating out from the pit. One breaks open between your legs and you jump aside just in time to avoid being swallowed. A large boulder on the top of the hill is teetering on the point of rolling down towards you. And as if that wasn't enough, a small green snake is wrapping itself around your ankle and preparing to bite you. What will you do first? Try to find an area safe from the cracking ground (turn to **6**), try to push the boulder off in a different direction (turn to **115**) or get rid of the snake (turn to **263**)?

44

A sudden gust grabs your pack, yanks it from your hands and sends it tumbling across the ground. It swirls about in the wind and comes open! You watch in dismay as the contents empty themselves from the pack. Covering your eyes, you dive out after the backpack and try to collect all your artefacts. But this is not easy. Even as you try to grab them, the wind is blowing them around and out of your reach. But you will recover anything in the pack which is not breakable (so you will lose vials of liquid, mirrors, etc.), except anything paper (for instance, maps or parchment scrolls), which will be blown away. Sort out your Equipment List and return to your crevice to wait for the dust storm to die down. Then turn to **10**.

45

The Serpent's hiss is a mocking laugh. 'Puny human!' it hisses. 'Do you think you can stick me with that small pin?' It darts down at you and the battle commences:

MOON SERPENT SKILL 13 STAMINA 10

If you kill the Serpent, turn to **62**.

46

The old Elf nods. He will take you to an empty caravan where you may sleep for the night, but the price will be 3 Gold Pieces. If you are prepared to pay this price, do so and follow him to the trailer (turn to **125**). If you do not wish to stay, you will have to leave the camp (turn to **294**).

47

It is mid-afternoon. Your long trek across Baddu-Bak is uneventful. You reach a spot where you may rest awhile and eat Provisions if you wish. If you would like to stop to eat, turn to **152**. If you would prefer to continue, turn to **95**.

48

For several hours you continue your trek across the barren Baklands. On the horizon, a solitary leafless tree appears and you head towards it. You may rest and take Provisions here and add 2 STAMINA points if this is your first meal of the day.

A noise in the branches disturbs you. You look up and hear a voice calling your name! High up in the branches, the bare twigs have formed themselves into a human face – an old man's face. And it's mouthing a message. The message drifts towards you: 'You seek the whereabouts of Shadrack of Baddu-Bak, that I know. To find him you must detour eastwards from your trail towards the Fishtail Rock. He is expecting you.' A breeze catches and disturbs the branches. When they settle, the face has disappeared!

Will you head east as the face advised (turn to **150**) or continue on the northward trail (turn to **94**)?

49

You may either draw your weapon and threaten the ferryman into taking you across for free, or try to outwit him with a magic spell:

FOG	GOD	LAW	DOC	FIX
404	480	332	441	379

If you choose to draw your weapon, the ferryman will fight with you:

FERRYMAN   SKILL 7   STAMINA 8

Once he has been reduced to a STAMINA of 4 or less, he will surrender and agree to take you across (turn to **110**).

50

How will the little creature react to your gift? Roll one die to decide.

If your gift is a spell artefact:

Die roll	
1	Turn to **33**
2–4	Turn to **22**
5–6	Turn to **290**

If your gift is something else:

Die roll	
1–3	Turn to **33**
4–5	Turn to **22**
6	Turn to **290**

51

The label on the vial certifies that the contents are waters from the holy springs in Daddu-Ley. Although you have no way of knowing this at the time, the water has not been blessed. It is ordinary river water and has no special powers at all. Turn to **86**.

52

The battle commences:

GOLDEN SNAKE   SKILL 6   STAMINA 6

The snake has a poisonous bite. If it inflicts any wounds on you before you kill it, roll one die to find out how many STAMINA points of damage the wound will cause. If you kill the snake, you may leave the area. Turn to **309**.

53

You prepare to cast your spell, keeping a careful eye on the Serpent. It darts this way and that, faster and faster until it is moving at an incredible pace. Watching the Serpent makes it difficult to concentrate on your spell and eventually you give up. You decide instead to use your weapon (turn to **103**), unless there is some alternative.

54

The battle commences:

EARTH SERPENT   SKILL 12   STAMINA 14

If you defeat the Serpent, turn to **220**.

55

You find a sheltered spot and settle down. If you wish to eat Provisions you may do so and you can add 2 STAMINA points if this is your first meal of the day (1 STAMINA point if you have already eaten). As you stretch out to sleep, you are aware of strange noises coming from the forest ahead. Strange animal calls haunt the air. What dangers lie in store for you? No doubt you will find out tomorrow. You drift off to sleep. Turn to **235**.

56
You quickly pray, and hope that Libra will hear you before it is too late. The pressure is becoming unbearable! But then the squeezing eases off. Libra has heard you! The leaves of the Stranglebush turn from their deep green colour to a dirty brown, and wilt on their branches. Your prayer has been answered – but you have used your one and only opportunity to gain help from Libra during this stage of your journey. Turn to **106**.

57
You call out loudly and wait. After ten minutes you try again. But there is no response. The area seems to be deserted. Will you try walking along the shoreline to see if you can find any signs of life (turn to **241**) or will you wait to see whether anyone finds *you* (turn to **233**)?

58

Quickly, you run after the Serpent, trying your best to keep it in sight. Like a burning branch suspended in the sky, it lights the way for you, but its speed is greater than yours. A wind has picked up and, to your relief, this is blowing more against the Serpent than you, allowing you to make up some ground. The wind whistles and swirls and you shield your face from the gusts. A gritty taste in your mouth raises the alarm. You are running into a sandstorm! You stop and watch the Serpent, holding your hands up to guard your eyes. It appears to be fighting a losing battle with the storm. Moments later a great swirling sandy gust blows up and the Serpent is unable to avoid it. Its flame flickers and is extinguished by the sand. As this happens, it starts to fall, plummeting down from the sky with your rucksack. Fighting against the wind, you fight on into the storm to catch your pack before its contents are smashed. It is tossed about in the storm, but you position yourself underneath, ready to catch it. Then, without warning, the Serpent comes crashing down on top of you, knocking you to the ground. Turn to **287**.

59

You read out the chant and the Serpent slows down. A pained expression comes over its face and it flaps its wings slowly. Its movements become sluggish and it hangs unnaturally in the air as if it should, by all rights, fall to the ground. But still it hangs there, slowly floating downwards. When it is within reach, you are able to attack it with your weapon:

SERPENT OF TIME   SKILL 3   STAMINA 14

If you defeat the creature, turn to **4**.

60

For several hours you march onwards until, in the distance, the line which forms the boundary of the Forest of the Snatta comes clearly into view. Overhead, the clouds rumble as they roll across the dark sky. You pause to consider how much further you must walk. The sudden sound of voices to your right startles you and you spin round. You rub your eyes and look again. Not twenty yards from where you stand, seven hooded shapes are squatting on the ground, playing some sort of game! Their bodies shimmer and you stare hard. You could swear that you can see *through* these bodies! And how could they appear from nowhere? For they were certainly not there seconds ago. One of them raises its head and turns towards you. Your eyes widen as the bony face of a long-dead skull opens its mouth. Its hollow voice whistles in the wind, calling your name: 'We have awaited your arrival. You have made good time, mortal. We are the Seven Spirits. We have been dispatched to warn you of the dangers ahead. Join us.'

Will you join them as you are invited (turn to **116**), or will you turn from them and set off towards the forest (turn to **82**)?

61

You back off and sweep round the caravan. You can see the camp guards following you round, but you are out of range of their arrows. When you reach the far side of the camp, you may continue. Turn to **269**.

62

The darkness disappears as the Serpent dies. You watch it lying on the ground and, before your eyes, it shrivels, coiling into a ball. Moments later, all that remains is a small Crystal Orb, which you may take with you. Turn to **285**.

63

You climb up on to the plinth and wander round the structure cautiously. It appears to be deserted. You call out, but there is no reply. Along one wall are some hieroglyphics which you may be able to decipher. In one corner you discover a trapdoor in the floor. Would you like to try to read the hieroglyphics (turn to **272**), open the trapdoor (turn to **180**) or keep looking (turn to **101**)?

64

The Horsemen take turns carrying you across the plains until you reach a ridge. Their leader tells you to dismount. 'Just over that ridge lives Manata, in a hole in the ground. We have no wish to meet his pets and will take you no further.' You climb down and thank them for the ride. As they disappear behind you, you climb up the ridge. Turn to **176**.

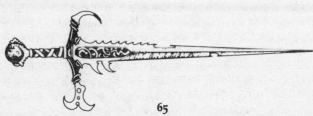

65

Behind you, the storm breaks. Again, the wind swells up, raising stones and earth with it. But you are on the fringe of the storm and will not feel its full wrath. Luckily, you have avoided it. Turn to **73**.

66

You grab at the Serpent, trying to hoist it into the air. You will lift the Serpent if you *Test your Luck* successfully and then roll a number less than your SKILL score with two dice. But each time you try this and fail to lift the Serpent, it will strike at you, causing 3 STAMINA points of damage (as you are undefended). If you lift the creature, turn to **127**. If you decide to stop trying, return to **263** and choose another attack.

67

Your choice will give you no advantage in fighting the Serpent. Draw your weapon and fight:

WATER SERPENT   SKILL 10   STAMINA 11

If you win, turn to **75**.

68

'Yes, yes, you must go. And quickly. For anyone who would threaten Fenestra is not welcome here. Begone!' You thank her and make your way back up to the door. Outside, you follow the path once more. Turn to **92**.

69

The old Elf stands up and nods. He will take you to an empty caravan where you may sleep for the night, but the price will be 3 Gold Pieces. If you will pay this price, do so and follow him to the trailer (turn to 125). If you cannot afford it, or you prefer not to pay, you will have to sit down again, pretend you are not too tired yet and either join in conversation with them (turn to 275) or ask to see their wares (turn to 315).

70

As you leap forward, the Horsemen release their bolts and three arrows fly towards you. Roll one die for each arrow. A roll of 1 or 2 indicates you are hit by that arrow for 2 STAMINA points of damage. Then you may resolve your battle. But if at least two of the arrows hit you, you must deduct 2 SKILL points during this battle:

First HORSEMAN	SKILL 8	STAMINA 7
Second HORSEMAN	SKILL 7	STAMINA 6
Third HORSEMAN	SKILL 7	STAMINA 8

Fight the Horsemen one at a time, in any order you wish. Once you have killed two of them (if you survive this long) and you have wounded the third at least twice, you may, if you wish, allow him to surrender (turn to 35). If you choose to kill all three, turn to 154.

71

As your blow lands, the creature yelps and leaps backwards. It licks its wound and turns to face you. Its eyes narrow and its mouth drops open, a low growl coming from its throat. Suddenly, it pounces! You realize its special power when in mid-flight it turns into a flaming ball and lands on you! Conduct the second Attack Round. If your Attack Strength is higher than its, then you successfully avoid the Fox and wound it. If its Attack Strength is higher, it will wound and scorch you for 5 STAMINA points of damage. After this second Attack Round, it will return to its normal self. The energy required to turn on its flame power will cost it 1 STAMINA and 1 SKILL point. Continue the battle to the death (remember it had an original SKILL of 7 and STAMINA of 6), but each time you wound it, it will turn on its flame power during the next Attack Round (repeat the procedure as above). If you kill it, turn to **95**.

72

He pleads with you: 'Have mercy, stranger! I will not harm you. Perhaps I can help you if you spare my life. What are you? A bandit? Here, have my gold! Or a warrior? Here, take this Chakram – its blade is deadly and its aim is true. Perhaps a wizard? I'll give you this magical powder for your spells. But leave me in peace!' You bend down to pick up his offerings. A money pouch contains 9 Gold Pieces. The Chakram is a sharp throwing disc. Before a fight starts, you may throw this at an enemy. When you do so, roll two dice. If you roll a number less than your SKILL, you will hit it for 2 STAMINA points of damage. His magical powder is yellow in colour and is contained in a small glass vial. You lower your weapon and speak to the man. You ask whether the Seven Serpents have been sighted in this area. 'Oh my, yes, yes. They flew over yesterday. In fact, one of them . . . er, one of them . . . ' His voice trails off and his eyes widen. 'Oh *no, no! Aaaiieeeeeee!*' You watch in amazement as he keels over backwards. Something has frightened him to death. Turn to **143**.

73

On and on you go, pausing briefly every now and again to scout out the land ahead. At one point you stop. Something is on the horizon! You squint ahead to try to make out the shape. It is definitely moving! You keep going and the shape becomes a little clearer. It is a small, two-legged creature about half your size and it has turned to come towards you. But it is moving at a remarkable rate! Do you want to continue to see what, or who, this is (turn to 162)? Otherwise you can head off in a different direction to avoid it (turn to 239)

74

Roll one die. This is the number of Snattacats that will spring to attack you. Each is identical, and they will attack you one at a time:

SNATTACAT   SKILL 7   STAMINA 9

These creatures can make themselves invisible at will. They will always be invisible when they start to attack and during the fight you must deduct 2 from your Attack Strength roll since you are fighting an invisible opponent. However, once you have inflicted a wound on a Snattacat, it will be dazed and the break in concentration will cause it to become visible again for one Attack Round (if it is not wounded again, it will make itself invisible). Your Attack Strength will be normal while you can see it. If you defeat all the Snattacats, turn to 160.

75

You catch your breath for a few moments, then set off towards the north shore of the lake. Half an hour later, you are pulling the boat up on to the marshy shore. You have crossed the lake. Turn to 147.

76

'I can tell you only that the Serpent of Time is the swiftest flier of the seven. And this Serpent can only be defeated by reciting a chant before it. But I have given this chant to the Marsh Goblins as they wish to kill the creature themselves. If you can find them, you may be able to persuade them to part with it. I hope this will be of help to you.' You thank her and prepare to leave. Turn to **324**. If you wish instead to ask for her advice on crossing Lake Ilklala, turn to **132**.

77

You struggle in vain to reach your weapon, as the Stranglebush tightens its grip. Gradually, the pressure increases. Turn to **305**.

78

You eat your meal and rest for a few moments. Add 2 STAMINA points if this is your first meal of the day, or 1 STAMINA point if you have already eaten. A short while later you pack up to leave. Turn to **300**.

79

'Ah, a *trader*, like ourselves, eh? Well, we like a good barter, don't we? Let's see what our friend has to offer.' The old Elf sits down and invites you to show them your wares. You may choose any artefact you wish to bargain for the food (except your weapon) and then you must test your bartering skills. Roll two dice. If the number rolled is lower than your SKILL, you manage to persuade them to accept it and you will be given a meal in exchange (turn to **163**). If the number is equal to or greater than your SKILL, then they will not accept it and you may repeat the procedure with another artefact. If you cannot, or will not, strike a bargain, turn to **288**.

80

Deduct one item from your Provisions. The Fox settles into your food, eating hungrily. With one eye, it watches you leave the rock and creep slowly off to continue your journey. Turn to **95**.

81

You find the snake-bite antidote and hold it ready in one hand as the Serpent poises to strike. Turn to **67**.

82

You turn away from them. 'Halt!' booms the ghostly voice. 'You shall not take another step northwards!' Will you stop as they command and wait to see what they have to say (turn to **116**) or will you ignore them and continue walking (turn to **140**)?

83

You march on. The featureless landscape offers little to attract your interest, but in the far distance you can make out the edge of the great forest you are heading towards. With luck you will reach it by nightfall. A chill wind sweeps across your path and makes you shiver momentarily. A short while later, another gust hits you with a force that almost knocks you over. Overhead, dark clouds are gathering and a rumbling noise rolls across the sky. But to the east and west you can see clear sky. *You* seem to be at the centre of the impending storm! Will you stop where you are and do what you can to make some shelter (turn to **308**), carry on regardless (turn to **247**) or head off in a north-westerly direction towards the clear sky (turn to **128**)?

84

Seeing you go for your weapon, the Deathwraith lets out a fearsome shriek and lunges at you. Resolve your battle with this creature:

DEATHWRAITH   SKILL 9   STAMINA 9

When you have reduced its STAMINA to 3 or less, turn to **205**.

85

You head on across the plain, keeping your eyes and ears open for warnings of danger. Suddenly the ground beneath you rumbles! You lose your footing and fall over on to your back. *Test your Luck*. If you are *Unlucky*, you have broken one item of your equipment (the most delicate one); if you are *Lucky*, nothing breaks. As you pick yourself up, you see the ground in front of you breaking up and two long claws emerge. The hole becomes larger and out of it crawls a giant BADDU-BEETLE. It turns towards you and advances. How will you fight it? With magic (turn to **191**) or with your weapon (turn to **286**)?

86

If you have bought any more artefacts from Oolooh, discover what they are by turning to the reference with the same number as the item. When you have done this, you may leave the caravan. You are greeted outside by the old Elf. Will you ask him for shelter for the night (turn to 46) or do you now wish to leave the camp (turn to 294)?

87

You show him the contents of your backpack. Do you have any Borrinskin boots with you? If so, turn to 184. If not, turn to 142.

88

The Orb is of clear crystal. You peer into it but can see nothing. It is heavy and, if an emergency arises, it would make a handy and quite dangerous missile. If you throw the Orb at a creature, you must roll lower than your SKILL with two dice to hit your target. If you succeed in hitting the creature, it will inflict 2 STAMINA points of damage. But if you hurl the Orb, you must also roll one die to check whether it breaks or not. If the roll is odd, it will shatter on impact. Turn to 86.

89

'So the Analander has the Serpent Ring!' hisses the Serpent as it hangs in the air. 'Then I must tell you that the Archmage is not as he seems, for this will warn you of his presence in Mampang. But you will never survive to reach the Fortress!' Return to 103.

90

You jump to the other side of the fallen tree and watch the space where you assume your attacker to be. A shape materializes in front of you. A furry beast, about the size of a large dog, appears. Its black fur is slashed with yellow flashes and its snub snout gives it an ugly appearance. But its large mouth reveals the danger – razor-sharp pointed teeth! The creature looks a little dazed from your blow but it looks around at you. Seeing that *you* can see *it*, it rises to its feet and closes its eyes, as if in concentration. The shape fades; it is once more invisible. You are on your guard, but a rustling in the undergrowth behind it suggests that it is leaving you. Laying down your weapon you look at your arm. It is painful, but not too seriously injured. You nurse it for a few moments, then pick up your weapon and pack to continue. Turn to 25.

91

You step forward out of cover and face the Goblins. Your sudden appearance takes them by surprise. What will your next step be? Will you draw your weapon (turn to **194**), try to talk with them (turn to **138**) or cast a spell?

GOB	NIF	POP	RAP	NIP
459	331	484	396	347

92

A little further along, the path divides into three. Will you take the left-hand path (turn to **244**), the right-hand path (turn to **274**) or the centre path (turn to **146**)?

93

The brass pendulum is exactly that: a small brass bob attached to a cord. Now turn to **86**.

94

You have been travelling for nearly a day. Will you settle down and sleep for the night or do you wish to keep awake, in case danger approaches while you can find no shelter? If you choose to sleep, turn to **16**. If not, turn to **122**.

95

You continue on into the early evening until it is difficult to see. Will you settle down to sleep for the night (turn to **224**) or walk on without rest (turn to **302**)?

96

You must cast your spell quickly, as the Serpent is attacking:

MAG	JIG	KID	HOT	FOG
413	405	392	377	364

If you know none of these, you must either draw your weapon (turn to **45**) or, if you have the means to make fire, turn to **155**. But your attempts at sorcery allow the Serpent to strike first – lose 2 STAMINA points unless you know one of the spells above.

97

Sheltering behind the rock, you may take the opportunity to eat Provisions. If you do so, add 2 STAMINA points if you have not yet eaten today, or 1 STAMINA point if you have. After a little while, the wind begins to die down. As you are preparing to leave, a strange whistling noise catches your attention. It is coming from the other side of the rock and you peer round cautiously to see what is happening. A strange sight greets your eyes. Whether a living creature or a freak of nature, you cannot be certain, but a swirling twist of air stands in a cove formed by the rock. It is like a miniature whirlwind, some three feet tall and two feet across. Perhaps it is trapped in the cove and is unable to spin its way out, or perhaps this object is alive and is sheltering or hiding in the rock. Do you wish to try to talk to it (turn to 267), ignore it and leave (turn to 322) or cast a spell?

RAP	HUF	MUD	HOW	YAP
421	359	389	446	490

98

In fact, the thump that you were expecting does not quite happen. Instead, your heart flutters as the short fall you anticipated lasts longer than it should. The ground below you has opened up and you have fallen into a pit resembling – perhaps appropriately – a freshly dug grave! But your landing is soft and you lift yourself back on your feet. The pit is around nine feet deep and you may just about be able to jump up and grab the edge to pull yourself up. As you are considering what to do, a creaking sound below puts you on your guard. The earth shakes in the centre of the pit and a rocky protrusion breaks through the surface. You stare at the smooth-faced rock and step backwards as a hissing sound comes from it. Its surface changes from grey to red and steam rises from it. This rock is boiling hot! In a panic you jump up to grab the rim of the pit and haul yourself out. Your fingers catch the edge but, as you pull yourself up, something bites your hand! This is not a serious wound, but it causes 1 STAMINA point of damage and makes you lose your grip. What will your next move be? Will you try again to lift yourself out of the pit (turn to 211), wait to see what happens in the pit (turn to 276) or cast a spell?

BAG	MUD	FOF	DOC	FIX
418	371	486	348	406

99

The four invisible cats approach. Although you cannot see them, you can hear their footsteps. The Snattacats will attack you one at a time. While they are invisible and hence difficult targets, you must deduct 2 points from your Attack Strength roll. However, as soon as you wound a Snattacat, this will cause it to break concentration and it will become visible for the next Attack Round. Resolve your battle. Each of the Snattacats is identical:

SNATTACAT   SKILL 7   STAMINA 9

If you defeat them, turn to 187.

100

You grab the pack and hold on. The Serpent flaps with its powerful wings and manages to lift both you and your pack into the air! It heads to the north and flies slowly off into the night. Meanwhile, you struggle to get a decent grip. It must be planning to take you towards Lake Ilklala! A blast of wind blows across the Serpent's path. This gust is so powerful that it all but douses the creature's flames and you are able to make out the Serpent's natural red body in the midst of the fire. But the blast was not a freak occurrence. You are now being taken by a tremendous wind, blowing you this way and that. A gritty taste in your mouth confirms your suspicions. You have flown straight into a sandstorm! You keep your eyes tightly shut, but you are aware that the Serpent is waging a tough struggle against the storm. You drop suddenly for an instant in the air until the creature resumes its grip. Again you drop, but this time for longer, and the fright forces you to open your eyes. Above you, the sand is damping the Serpent's fire and it is flapping frantically to keep aloft! You fall faster and faster! The Serpent's flame goes out and it follows you down, down, down through the air. With a great thump, you land on the ground. Turn to 287.

101

There seems to be little else of interest in the building. Will you try to read the hieroglyphics (turn to **272**), investigate the trapdoor (turn to **180**), go outside and have a look at the well (turn to **23**) or leave the area (turn to **309**)?

102

You wait for hours, peering across the dark Baklands. The strain of your ordeal is tremendous and your strength begins to fade. Soon you are unable even to think clearly and consciousness fades. The carrion crows above you, circling and cawing, will soon alight on the cross to ensure that you never awake. Your mission has ended.

103

As you pull out your weapon, the Serpent strikes! But something strange has happened. You saw it start to move; and you can see it now hovering, with blood dripping from its fangs – but you saw nothing in between! Slowly, pain arises in your arm. The pain steadily increases until it is unbearable and you cannot stop yourself calling out. Your mouth opens to call and your head turns to see your wound. To your horror you realize that you are moving and reacting at a fraction of your normal speed! A deep wound on your arm is bleeding, but the blood is seeping from it unnaturally slowly and each drop falls to the ground like a feather. When your shout of pain eventually comes from your lips it is a low growl. What is happening? Your head turns to look up at the Serpent. The creature is darting about in the sky watching you and waiting for its moment to pounce again. Suddenly its tongue is again licking bloody fangs. It has struck again! But this time, its bite was not to your arm. Instead the pain slowly comes from your neck. As the pain dawns on you, so consciousness fades. This is a wound from which you will not recover. The Serpent of Time has claimed another victim.

104

The sight in front of you appears to be a Deathwraith and you step forward cautiously. Deathwraiths are powerful, undead creatures. It is still beckoning you with its finger, but as you approach, it spreads its arms wide to clasp you. You must act quickly. What will you do:

Draw out a silver weapon?	Turn to **84**
Draw out a normal weapon?	Turn to **32**
Prepare to cast a spell?	Turn to **310**

105

You wait for a while, but nothing comes. You decide instead to head on cautiously in the direction from which the Goblins came. Turn to **295**.

106

You step out of the Stranglebush and brush yourself down. The path leads onwards, running slightly downhill. You pass through a small clearing where you stop and look. Through the trees you can see the next stage of your journey – Lake Ilklala. You must cross the lake to reach the foothills of Xamen, from where the uphill journey will take you to the Fortress at Mampang. But you are wasting time. You set off once more through the woods until you reach a fork. Will you take the left-hand path (turn to **119**) or the right-hand path (turn to **274**)?

107

Walking into the wind is extremely tiring. Deduct 1 STAMINA point. Which way are you heading? To the north-west (turn to **149**) or the north-east (turn to **73**)?

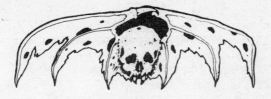

108

He seems to take your refusal as some sort of insult and raises his pipe to his mouth. You may cast a spell:

PEP	JIG	FAR	SUS	KID
427	353	450	408	388

Or you may wait to see what happens (turn to **248**).

109

You have rightly deduced that this creature is one of the Serpents. Calling to it in the branches, you hold up the ring. The Serpent coils and hisses at you. 'So!' it says. 'You have found the Serpent Ring. I am bound by that ring to reveal to you a secret which will be useful to you. But after that I will kill you! Very well, Analander, I can tell you this: eat not from the larder of Throg if your journey should cause you to meet her. But you will never reach Throg's larder. I will see to that!' Now return to **123** to make your choice.

110

He disappears into the undergrowth and reappears a few moments later dragging a heavy boat. 'Give me a hand, idiot!' he barks, and together you pull the boat into the water and climb in. He throws you the oars and snaps, 'Take the oars, fool, and start rowing.' Somehow his manner has changed and his tone is more aggressive. Will you do as he says (turn to **293**) or are you not going to take orders from someone whose job it is to row *you* across (turn to **223**)?

111

'Ho there, stranger,' says their leader. 'We are Baklands Horsemen. What is your purpose in Baddu-Bak?' You tell them you are heading for the Forest of the Snatta and will cause them no harm. One of them whispers something about seeing whether you carry any valuables. Will you hold your ground and wait for their next move (turn to **257**) or draw your weapon (turn to **313**)?

112

The mumblings continue. The old Elf steps forward. 'All right then, stranger,' he says. 'Perhaps our wares may tempt you, for we are a trading caravan. Let us show you what we have to offer. Follow me.' You follow him out of the kitchen tent. Turn to **315**.

113

You may either run off in a north-westerly direction (turn to **174**) or take a wide detour round the creature and continue northwards (turn to **170**).

114

Which way will you now head? To the north-west (turn to **149**), or northwards (turn to **283**)? You may rest and eat Provisions, if you wish, and if you do so you will gain 2 STAMINA points if this is your first meal today or 1 STAMINA point if you have already eaten.

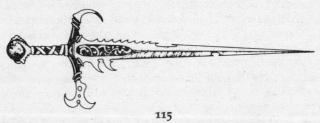

115

You climb up the incline towards the boulder, which is now dangerously close to losing its balance. The little snake on your leg strikes, digging in its fangs and making you wince in pain. Deduct 2 STAMINA points. You pause to rub your wound and, as you do so, the ground cracks beneath you. You fall down into a crevice which closes slightly and traps your leg! Frantically you pull, but your leg is held fast, and your heart sinks as you feel your foot heating up. One of the glowstones has appeared beneath it! You must think quickly and either cast a spell:

ZAP	FAR	YOB	FOF	SUN
462	438	362	390	375

or call on help from Libra (turn to **158**). If you can do neither of these, the only course of action left will not be pleasant. You may only free yourself by cutting off your leg! If you are forced to choose this option, turn to **186**.

116

Who *are* these creatures? And who has sent them? Do they offer advice, or are they dangerous? The spirits rise as you approach. They glide silently through the air, passing right through one another as they mingle. You now stand in the centre of their ring and watch as they link hands to surround you. Again the ghostly voice speaks to you: 'Your caution is understandable. But fear us not. These are not our natural bodies but merely the shells through which we communicate with mortals. We wish to help. In these bodies we cannot touch you. But we can give you knowledge. There are dangers ahead the likes of which you cannot imagine. But we know a magical chant which will protect you from harm.' Do you wish to hear this chant? If so, turn to **166**. Otherwise you may ask them to reveal their true selves to you (turn to **323**) or you may make plans for leaving (turn to **207**).

117

Further along the path, you stop as a red-coloured snake slides across the path. It sees you and stops. The two of you stare at each other for a few seconds and the snake resumes its journey. Do you wish to leave the path and follow the snake (turn to 226), or will you press on with your own journey (turn to 306)?

118

Desperately you grab at the side of the boat and in the nick of time you find something to hold on to. The boat tosses about for a short while, then steadies itself. The waters go calm. An unnatural stillness hangs in the air. You have the feeling that something even more dangerous is about to happen. Turn to 303.

119

The path winds tortuously through the forest. At one stage it skirts a hillock and a sound makes you stop. Some inner sense advises caution as you proceed and creep forward slowly around the hillock. On the far side is a wooden doorway. Sounds from within indicate that someone or something is definitely inside. Do you want to creep up to the door to see what is going on (turn to 171) or will you tiptoe past and continue along the path (turn to 92)?

120

You rise and collect your things together, listening carefully for any other suspicious sounds. You hear one! A soft, deep-throated growling is coming from something not more than a few feet from you. But there is nothing there! The growl grows into a roar and something fires itself through the air and fastens itself on your arm! Still you can see nothing; an invisible animal has gripped your arm with powerful jaws. The blood is seeping through your tunic. You pull out your weapon and bring it down heavily on what must be the head of the animal. It howls and releases its grip, allowing you to race off along the path. But you must deduct 3 STAMINA points for your injury. Turn to **271**.

121

He considers for a moment, then nods his head. 'Perhapsss we can do some businessss,' he says. He scrapes some earth away from the wall of the pit and pulls out a sack, offering you a vial of liquid. 'Thiss iss Holy Water from Daddu-Yadu,' he says. He will exchange it with you for any two items from your backpack (but not Gold or Provisions). Exchange if you wish and then leave by turning to **318**. If you wish to try to rob the Snake Charmer of the Holy Water and his Bamboo Pipe, you will have to pretend to leave and then leap on him with your sword from the top of the pit (turn to **218**).

122

You continue through the night. Lose 2 STAMINA points for going without sleep and another 3 STAMINA points if you did not eat at all yesterday. Continue by turning to **230**.

123

You approach the tree and stare up into the branches, searching for the snake. You catch a glimpse of red up there, but something is not quite right. The thick red band you have seen could not possibly belong to the small snake you were following. Then it happens . . . without warning, the upper part of the tree bursts into flame! A flash-fire billows out from the tree. Before you can take evasive action, flames lick at you. You cannot stop yourself crying out as the fire singes your hair and eyebrows. Roll one die. A roll of 1–4 indicates the singeing damage: deduct this number of STAMINA points. A roll of 5 or 6 affects your eyes: deduct 3 STAMINA points and 1 SKILL point. But just as suddenly as it began, the fire goes out, leaving a badly charred tree. The burnt foliage allows you to see up into the branches, where the snake is looking down at you. It has grown tenfold in size and two wings are folded on its back. Its sly eyes are watching you as if it were deciding its next trap. Will you draw your weapon and climb the tree to face it (turn to **42**), or cast a spell?

HUF	NIF	HOT	FAL	ZAP
474	434	411	336	460

Or do you have something else in mind (turn to **197**)?

124

The ring has a small pearl mounted in it. You paid a fair price for what is a fine piece of jewellery. If you ever wish to sell or barter it, it will be worth 10 Gold Pieces. Turn now to **86**.

125

The inside of the trailer is fairly clean and you bed down for the night. You awake early next morning. Add 3 STAMINA points for your rest. Did you eat at all yesterday? If not, you must lose 3 STAMINA points as you are now hungry. As you still do not trust the Black Elves entirely, you decide to creep off in the early-morning light. Will you head on a long north-westward trek (turn to **47**), march off in a north-north-westerly direction (turn to **15**) or head north-eastwards (turn to **73**)?

126

You reach out with your hand to feel the suction above the top of the whirlwind. The force is quite strong. Without warning, the whistling sound increases in pitch dramatically and the thing swirls at a tremendous speed. The force on your hand catches you unawares and you lurch forward. In a split second you are trapped! Whatever it is has sucked you inside so quickly that you lose consciousness before you realize what has happened. Your inquisitive nature has cost you your mission – and your life . . .

127

The Serpent roars and hisses as you lift it into the air. But once off the ground, its power is lost. The living earth settles and the Serpent itself shrinks once more to the size of the small snake. Grabbing it by the neck, it is an easy matter for you to destroy the beast. Turn to **220**.

128

You march on smartly, trying to avoid the storm before it can build up. Roll two dice and compare the total with your SKILL score. If your roll is lower than your SKILL score, turn to **65**. If the roll is equal to or higher than your SKILL, turn to **328**.

129

As you hold up the ring, the Serpent hisses loudly, 'Foolish adventurer, your ring will not protect you from my wrath. Your death is certain. But by its power I must reveal to you my secret. Four guards protect the entrance to the Fortress of Mampang. But this information will do you no good, for you will never reach the High Fortress.' Now return to **143** to deal with the Serpent.

130

The Serpent Ring you were given will be an invaluable item in this part of your journey, for it has power over the Archmage's Serpents. If you confront the Serpents while wearing this ring, you can command them to reveal useful information. You can do this in the following way:

At certain references when you confront a Serpent (these references will all end in a number 3), you may command the Serpent to reveal its information by deducting 14 from the reference number you are on and turning to this reference. If you wish to do this, you must remember this instruction, as no option will be given in the text. If you do not have the Serpent Ring, you are forbidden from discovering this information and you should not be reading this reference now.

131

The Serpent agrees to your terms. You replace the skin and the creature flies down as if to re-enter its body. But instead of keeping its bargain, the Serpent nips across to you and wraps its wispy body around your face! You cough and gasp as your lungs take in the pungent gas. You struggle to free yourself from its grip, but it is no use: the Serpent is firmly locked in place. You slump down. Moments later you are unconscious; minutes later you will be dead. More fool you for trusting one of the Seven Serpents!

132

'Crossing Ilklala?' she asks. 'It can be crossed but only if you are able to summon the ferrymaster. I have here a whistle which you may blow to call him. For this whistle I will ask only 2 Gold Pieces. Or I will exchange it for anything you may have which will be useful to me.' You may exchange any of your spell artefacts for the whistle, but she is not interested in any non-magical items. Exchange, if you wish, and then turn to **324**.

133

As you reach the forest, the air is becoming cooler and night is approaching. You must decide whether to camp on the outskirts of the forest for the night or to carry on without resting. If you wish to stop to eat and rest, turn to **55**. If you would rather carry on through the night, turn to **159**.

134

The little creature is asking for a gift as a token of friendship. Will you give it something? If you do, it must be something fairly valuable (not food or a useless object). If you choose to give it a gift, turn to **50**. If you do not wish to give valuable presents to complete strangers, you can refuse (turn to **210**).

135

You run forward but must jump aside quickly to avoid being hit by a falling pillar. A large rock lands on your shoulder and causes you another 2 STAMINA points of damage. The whole building is now shaking and your escape route has been cut off! Soon the roof will collapse on you! You must think quickly to find a way to avoid certain death. Will you:

Return to the hieroglyphics and keep reading?	Turn to **164**
Pray to Libra for assistance?	Turn to **320**
Pray to this new goddess for mercy?	Turn to **206**

136

You crouch down in a clump of reeds to wait for your visitors to arrive. A few minutes later, a small group of Marsh Goblins, ugly snub-nosed creatures with webbed hands, arrive in the clearing and stop. They are panting hard as if they are being chased. They jabber at one another, but you cannot understand their language. Will you wait until they have moved on (turn to **292**) or step forward and reveal yourself to them (turn to **91**)?

137

A few hundred yards ahead of you is a camp of covered wagons and carts, arranged in a circle. A fire burns in the centre, and you can see bodies moving around the camp. You walk towards the caravan. Your approach is noticed and an arrow flies through the air, landing to your left. Another lands to your right. Will you hold your hands in the air to show them you mean no harm (turn to **259**) or retrace your steps and take a wide detour round the camp (turn to **61**)?

138

You try a few words of greeting, but they cannot understand you. Instead they shout at you in a language you do not understand – unless you know an interpretation spell. Return to **91** and choose again.

139

The Bear rises on to two legs and advances. Its sharp teeth and claws are dangerous weapons. Resolve your combat:

WILD BEAR   SKILL 8   STAMINA 8

If you defeat the creature, turn to **20**.

140

As you suspected, their threatening tone was merely to frighten you. Their lifeless bodies posed no real threat to you. Several yards further on you glance behind at them. They have disappeared! You continue your path towards the next stage of your quest: the Forest of the Snatta. Turn to **133**.

141

Stones and small rocks have been swept up in the dust storm. As you shelter in your crevice holding your head in your hands, you stand a chance of being injured by the swirling debris. *Test your Luck*. If you are *Lucky*, you escape injury. If you are *Unlucky*, you must lose 2 STAMINA points for your injuries. Then you must wait until the dust storm subsides. Turn to **10**.

142

He is not interested in anything in your pack and picks up his pipe once more. Do you wish to stay, watch him and perhaps ask him if he can help you (turn to **7**) or will you now leave the pit (turn to **318**)?

143

In an instant, your world goes black, as if the sun had been snuffed out like a candle. A hissing sound gets louder and louder and a glowing moon appears above you. The round shape suddenly uncoils itself and a great shimmering Moon Serpent hovers in the air above you on glistening wings. It is poised and ready to strike! Will you:

Draw your weapon?	Turn to **45**
Cast a spell?	Turn to **96**
Or do you have the means to make fire?	Turn to **155**

144

You continue through the night. Eerie noises float across the countryside and you are glad you decided to continue. But as dawn approaches, your lack of sleep is affecting you. Lose 2 STAMINA points and another 3 STAMINA points if you did not eat at all yesterday. You march on. Turn to **11**.

145

You climb down the stairs. 'I don't believe it! I don't believe my eyes! Another human!' stammers the man, excitedly. 'Oh, stranger, please release me from my shackles and let me live once again in the world of light!' He is chained to the wall by his ankle. The chain is thin and would shatter easily from a weapon's blow. But you are a little suspicious and ask him first of all how he came to be chained up beneath this place. 'It was Klattamen. Damned Klattamen!' he curses. '*They* were the ones who ransacked this temple, took everything of value and left me, Throff's own priest – my name is Shalla, by the way – chained up. A prisoner in my own temple!' His story seems genuine enough. Will you release him as he requests (turn to 40) or leave him there (turn to 262)?

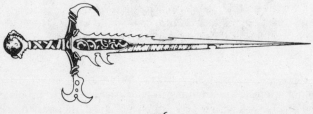

146

You reach a clearing where you can stop to rest and eat. If you wish to take Provisions here, you can add 2 STAMINA points if you have not yet eaten today or 1 STAMINA point if you have already had a meal. When you have finished, turn to 20.

147

You tie the boat up in a sheltered spot and wade through the Vischlami Swamp. *Test your Luck*. If you are *Lucky*, turn to 182. If you are *Unlucky*, turn to 253.

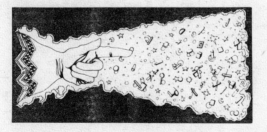

148

Carefully hiding your sand from the creature, you climb the tree. As it sees you climb, it drops from the branches on to the ground below. Quickly, you scamper down, before the creature can create its fire again. On the ground, you face each other, waiting for a move. In an instant, the Serpent bursts into flames and stretches its wings. Quickly, you throw your sand at it. The creature squeals and screams as the sand covers it. The flames go out. The wings disappear. Before you is the small yellow snake you were following originally! You draw out your weapon and finish it off:

SNAKE   SKILL 5   STAMINA 6

If you kill the snake, turn to **306**.

149

The great forest ahead of you is now less than an hour's walk away; your trek across the Baklands is almost over. But ahead of you, barring your way, is a small village. Loosely grouped huts made from branches and foliage suggest that the inhabitants are fairly primitive. Do you want to enter the village (turn to **19**) or will you take a north-easterly detour away from it (turn to **283**)?

The Fishtail Rock comes into view a little further on. It is well named, with two peaks, as if a huge fish were half buried on the plain. A fire burns outside the entrance to a small cave. You call out to attract the occupant of this dwelling-place and an old man shuffles out. You recognize the face of the tree spirit! This must be Shadrack himself.

'I have been expecting you,' he says in greeting. 'I know of your journey from Kharé. Be it folly or bravery which takes you across the Baklands, I must warn you that none of Analand have crossed Kakhabad alone and survived. Come, let us chat by the warmth of the fire. I may be of some help to you. And for my part I wish to know what is happening in the Cityport.'

For some time you talk, telling him news of the outside world. He offers you a meal, which you may take, adding 2 STAMINA points if you have not yet eaten today (or 1 STAMINA point if you have). You are anxious to know of the messengers of Mampang.

'Ah, the Seven Serpents,' he starts. 'Indeed, they are in the Baklands, but I knew not that it was news of your journey that they carried back to Mampang. Let me tell you what I know of them, for they are no friends of mine.

'Legend has it that some twelve years ago, the Archmage of Mampang fought and slew a mighty Hydra which dwelt in the caves of High Xamen. So formidable a foe was this creature that the Archmage took its seven heads to Mampang where he used his black arts to resurrect them as seven winged serpents. They became his personal messengers and, as an act of faith, he assigned each to one of his own gods. In return, the gods bestowed their own powers on these foul creatures to aid the Archmage. The power of the sun was bestowed on the Sun Serpent, as was the moon on the Moon Serpent. Earth, water, fire and air became powers of four more Serpents and the last, the Serpent of Time, was given perhaps the greatest power. But each has its own weakness. Discover these weaknesses and you may defeat the creatures, but otherwise no mortal stands a chance against their powers. The Serpents keep knowledge of their own vulnerabilities as their closest secrets. I myself know only one: the Air Serpent may leave its body and become a puff of gas. But while in this state it will die unless it is able to re-enter its body within minutes. Destroy its unprotected body and you destroy the creature.'

It is now late. You may spend the night in Shadrack's cave and add 3 STAMINA points. Next morning you can set off again. Before you go, Shadrack offers you an ornate Galehorn to aid you on your journey. Will you now set off northwards (turn to **85**) or rejoin the main trail (turn to **230**)?

151

'Oh, yes,' he continues. 'We may be able to arrange for you to meet the Seven Serpents. And . . .' – he snaps his fingers behind his back – ' . . . and sooner than you think! *Guards!*' In an instant, five strong Black Elves are holding you. You try to reach for your weapon, but you cannot move your arms. 'Yes,' laughs the old Elf. 'Let's arrange for our friend to meet the Seven Serpents!' The guards bind your hands and set to work making a tall wooden cross. They tie your arms and ankles securely to the cross, nail a black flag to the top, and set it firmly into the ground leaving you hanging high up in the air. You are powerless to prevent them. Below you, the Black Elves are laughing and jeering. 'Let the Archmage know who has delivered his enemy!' proclaims the old Elf. 'We will get our just reward!' A short while afterwards, the caravan packs up to leave, while you hang limply – and painfully – on your cross. Lose 4 STAMINA points. When they have gone, you may either wait to see what fate has in store for you (turn to **102**) or, if you are able, call on your goddess for help (turn to **243**).

152

You eat your food. If this is your first meal today, add 2 STAMINA points. If you have already eaten, add 1 STAMINA point. You sit on a bare rock and stare into the wilderness ahead of you, your thoughts fixed on the Forest of the Snatta, which you must pass through. You become aware of a scratching noise on the other side of the rock and lean forward. Two dark eyes are staring at you! With a sudden leap, a red-furred Fox jumps out of its hole and faces you. Evidently your food has attracted it. Will you throw it some food (turn to **80**), cast a spell (turn to **179**) or draw your weapon to attack it (turn to **256**)?

153

The suit of chainmail fits you perfectly. You may wear this from now on and it will help protect you in battles. You may add 1 SKILL point while you are wearing this armour and, if you are wounded in a battle, the Chainmail may help minimize the damage. Roll 1 die after each wound. If you roll a 5 or 6, the Chainmail will absorb most of the blow (deduct 1 STAMINA point only instead of the normal 2). If you roll a 1 to 4, the damage will be as normal. Turn now to **86**.

154

You pause to rest after the battle. While doing so, you go through the Horsemen's possessions. You find 4 Gold Pieces, a pouch containing fine brown sand and a mass of green fur. On further inspection, this turns out to be a wig. You may keep all of these and then set off once more. Turn to **273**.

155

Have you collected a tinderbox or flash-fire powder along your journey? Or any other means of making fire? If so, you may create a fire to burn the Serpent. Fire is the Moon Serpent's weakness. With fire as your weapon, you may fight it as:

MOON SERPENT   SKILL 7   STAMINA 6

If you defeat the Serpent, turn to **62**.

156

You rush over to the trapdoor and heave it open. Steps lead downwards and, at the bottom . . . 'Aaaiiiiiieeee!' Two voices shriek loudly. One is your own, but whose is the other? At the foot of the stairs is a thin, half-naked old man with long grey hair and a beard. 'Quickly!' he screams. 'Shout "Throff". And repeat it three times! Hurry!' You do as he asks and within moments the temple is still once more. You breathe a sigh of relief and turn to thank the old man. Turn to **145**.

157

You creep up to it slowly until you are less than three feet away. It does not flinch, but remains in position, spinning quickly. You watch it for a short while, trying to make out what it is, but it is still a mystery. A small fly buzzes over the whirlwind and is sucked into it but it seems to be totally uninterested in its surroundings. Do you wish to touch it (turn to **126**) or will you leave it be and continue your journey (turn to **322**)?

158

Quickly, you mouth a silent prayer to your goddess. The pain in your foot becomes sharper (lose 3 STAMINA points) but you sigh in relief as the ground around you creaks and the pressure is released. Your goddess has come to your aid! Your foot frees itself and a small voice whispers in your ear: 'My loyal subject. I may save you this once in the Baklands but you are now on your own until the Fortress at Mampang. I leave you with this word of advice. Your present troubles are caused by the Earth Serpent. Destroy it by raising it into the air; for its power comes from the earth itself.' Do you now wish to leave this area as quickly as possible (turn to **165**) or do you wish to look for the Earth Serpent (turn to **307**)?

159

The going is slow as you pick your way through the forest in the dark. You begin by following a trail, but it is difficult to see in the moonless night and you soon lose the path. You may stop along the way to eat Provisions (add STAMINA points if you do: 2 points if you have not eaten today or 1 point if this is not your first meal). If you have not eaten during the day, you must lose 3 STAMINA points as you are now very hungry. You must also lose 2 STAMINA points for going without sleep. Eventually light returns with the dawn. You have not made good progress but after searching round for half an hour, you manage to find the path again. Turn to **13**.

160

You rest for a moment and then decide it prudent to leave as quickly as possible. You set off, following the trail. Turn to **271**.

161

At the mention of the Seven Serpents, his eyes narrow and he scowls at you. The tune he is playing becomes faster and his pet snakes slither towards you. Turn to **202**.

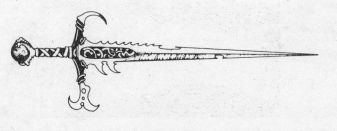

162

You allow your visitor to approach. As it gets closer, you can see that it is a small, gnome-like creature with dark skin and ugly features. Its little legs move at an incredible rate and it helps itself along with a walking stick carved to resemble a serpent. It stops in front of you and you both look at each other. Silently you wonder whether this is a friend or a foe. 'Have it whichever way you like!' says the creature in a squeaky voice. 'If it's "friend", then show me your friendship. Give me a gift of greeting! Or if it's "foe", then begone! Get out of my way!' Will you treat the little creature as a friend (turn to **134**) or foe (turn to **210**)?

163

The Whortle soup is hot and nourishing. It is a creamy-grey vegetable soup. It sometimes has a strange effect on people who have not eaten it before. Roll one die. If you roll a 1–5, turn to **231**. If you roll a 6, turn to **18**.

164

You creep carefully over to the wall which bore the fateful inscription. But much of the writing has now been destroyed. However, the end of the message is still intact. It reads: '. . . Death will be certain unless the victim will chant the goddess's name thrice loudly.'

Do you remember the goddess's name? If so, repeat it three times loudly and turn to **9**. If you cannot remember her name, you will have to either pray to Libra (turn to **320**) or ask this goddess for mercy (turn to **206**). *You can check the goddess's name at reference* **189** *– but you are on your honour to do this* after *you have repeated it.*

165

Ahead of you, perhaps an hour's walk away, are the fringes of the Forest of the Snatta, the next stage of your journey. After a brief rest, you collect yourself and set off towards it. Turn to **133**.

166

'Very well,' whispers the voice. 'Listen carefully and repeat this incantation after me:

> *Arbil Madarbil*
> *I offer a sign;*
> *Arbil Madarbil*
> *No idol of mine.*
>
> *Though, Arbil Madarbil,*
> *I worship you not,*
> *Let fortune o'ersee me,*
> *Let luck be my lot.'*

Will you repeat this verse as the spirit suggests (turn to **297**) or not (turn to **3**)?

167

Test your Luck. If you are *Lucky*, turn to **27**. If you are *Unlucky*, turn to **77**.

168

You quickly dart off into the reeds and are relieved to find that the Goblins are not interested in following you. Instead they set off in the direction they were originally heading. You continue under cover of the swamp. Turn to **295**.

169

You look into the Orb and hold your Serpent Ring up to the trapped creature. 'A curse on you, human!' it hisses. 'I am trapped, but I will be freed. And when I am, your journey will have been wasted.' Again you hold up the ring and demand that the Sun Serpent reveals its secret. 'I am compelled to give you one piece of advice, and this is it: beware the breath of the Mucalytics. But I will tell you no more.' Return to **183**.

170

You continue for several hours until the darkness of night spreads across the land. But shelter is nowhere to be found. Will you bed down for the night to rest and eat (turn to **225**) or would you prefer to keep going through the night (turn to **255**)?

171

You cannot see anything through the door. You will have to either leave the area (turn to 92), or open the door (turn to 265). If you wish to enter, you may want to cast a spell first:

TEL	DOP	POP	ZAP	FAR
425	469	399	409	354

172

You may either draw your weapon and battle the creature:

WATER SERPENT   SKILL 10   STAMINA 11

Or you may look through your backpack for something to use (turn to 245). If you choose to fight the Serpent and you win, turn to 75.

173

The creatures appear to be most annoyed that you refuse their hospitality. They shout angrily after you in a series of grunts. But no one stops you. In fact they seem to be more engrossed in their own arguments than they are concerned with you! You walk on, leaving them squabbling senselessly with one another. Leaving the village, you are a short distance from the next stage of your journey: the Forest of the Snatta. Turn to 133.

174

As you run, the world blacks out in an instant, as if the sun were snuffed out like a candle. The screeching noise becomes a softer hissing sound as it fades into the distance. You glance behind to see a single glowing ball above you in the sky, which fades. As it dies, daylight returns. You stop and head off in a north-westerly direction until you see something that makes you stop. Turn to 137.

175

Your movement causes them to retaliate hastily. Three arrows shoot towards you at dangerously close range. Throw one die for each arrow. A roll of 1–3 is a hit, for 3 STAMINA points of damage. If all three hit you, you are seriously wounded – turn to **325**. If two, one or none of the arrows hit you, you may still cast your spell (after taking the STAMINA damage):

ROK	DIM	FAL	DOP	SAP
495	391	445	476	422

If you know none of these, turn to **70**.

176

A strange musical wailing sound reaches your ears as you approach a natural pit in the ground. You approach cautiously and peer over the edge. Down below is a thin, dark-skinned man squatting on the ground and playing a pipe. In front of him, half a dozen snakes are writhing in the air and watching him. Do you wish to shout down to him (turn to **200**) or leap down into the pit with your weapon at the ready (turn to **218**)? If you would prefer, you could sneak away quietly instead (turn to **318**).

177

The Horn is, in fact, an ornate Galehorn with the power of the wind. But its power is only available to those who have been trained in sorcery! Turn now to **86**.

178

Which spell will you use?

WAL	FOG	LAW	FIX	MUD
337	380	430	463	483

If you know none of these, you will have to draw your weapon. Turn to **258**.

179

Which spell will you cast?

GUM	NIF	FOG	HOT	YAP
497	400	468	349	416

If you know none of these, you may either throw it some food (turn to 80) or draw your weapon (turn to 256).

180

You grasp the trapdoor handle and test its weight. With a good heave you should be able to lift it. Using all your strength, you manage to lift it and then flip it over on its hinges. A few steps lead downwards and the smell below is disgusting. As the light floods in, you can see *something* down there, but you can't make out what. It could be something alive, but . . . 'Aaaaiiieeeee!' Two voices (one of them your own!) scream in fright as your eyes meet. At the foot of the steps is a skinny, half-naked old man with long wild hair and a beard. You step back to compose yourself after the shock. Do you want to climb down the stairs to see who this is (turn to 145) or leave the building (turn to 309)?

181

You protest, and the little creature looks on you in disbelief. 'Look, Analander, I've told you once, and I'm telling you again. I don't care if your pride *is* wounded! That's nothing to the wound I'll give you across your throat if you don't stand aside to let an old lady pass.' The creature reaches out with its stick and touches your weapon. It turns into a twisting snake! You knock it on to the floor. As you jump aside, the ugly little creature walks past. You watch it go in amazement. When it is some distance off, your weapon returns to normal. You pick it up and continue. Turn to 114.

182

Eventually the water becomes shallow and you step out on to marshy ground. You find a spot where you may rest and eat Provisions if you wish. If you wish to stop and eat, add 2 STAMINA points if you have not yet eaten today or 1 point if you have. As you get ready to leave, you hear a crashing in the distance, followed by cries. Something – or a group of somethings – is heading your way. Will you stay where you are but hide (turn to **136**), run away in the opposite direction (turn to **270**) or wait to see what happens (turn to **316**)?

183

You are getting on well with her and decide to bring the conversation round to your mission. You ask her about the Seven Serpents. She stops talking and looks at you, her eyes widening. 'What interest have you in the Seven Serpents?' she asks. Dare you risk telling her the truth? You decide to play safe and tell her you have heard they are about and you would like to set eyes on these infamous creatures. 'I can lead you to one of the creatures,' she says, 'for I have a secret. I believe I can trust you with it. The Seven Serpents are no friends of mine, for each time they fly out into Kakhabad, they land in this forest, causing disturbances. The cursed Water Serpent killed my father during one such visit. This I shall never forget. My father did not know of its weakness, for the Serpent of Water cannot abide oil. Oil and water do not mix and for this reason I have a plentiful store. For I will avenge my father. But let me show you what I have in my Orb.' Realizing that you have found a useful ally, you explain to Fenestra that you must kill these creatures. She smiles. 'Then take this flask of oil with you on your journey. And may your goddess be with you if you meet the evil creature.' She hands you a flask of oil and turns to the Glass Orb on the table. Then she smooths her hands over the surface, mumbling under her breath. A shape begins to appear in the Orb. Your jaw drops as you make out the form of a winged serpent. 'Yes,' she says, 'I have here the Sun Serpent, lured down from the skies with a Rain Spell. I offered it shelter – for the Sun Serpent cannot tolerate water – and magicked it into my Orb. Eventually, the Water Serpent will come looking for its companion and when that happens, I will be ready. Look, you can talk to the creature if you wish.' She looks deep into the Orb with a look of disgust on her face. You may now ask her for advice on crossing Lake Ilklala (turn to **132**), or ask her for any other advice she may have on the Serpents (turn to **76**), or you may leave and rejoin the path (turn to **92**).

184

'Oooh, yesss,' cries the Snake Charmer. 'Manata likesss shoesss. I wantss them!' He claims that he can give you valuable information if you will give him the shoes. You ask what sort of information. He whispers, 'The Sseven Sserpentsss.' Do you wish to take him up on his offer (turn to 228) or would you prefer to hang on to the boots (turn to 108)?

185

You run over to the rock and crouch in its folds, hiding from the undead creature. Its eyes follow you and again it laughs loudly. Holding its bony hands in front of it, it raises them slowly into the air. You wait in anticipation. Seconds later, a deep rumbling sound shakes the earth and you panic! The rocks around you are moving! You try desperately to spring from the rocks, but your leg has been caught in a fold. The rock is coming alive! Helplessly, you watch as a great Rock Demon rises from the ground and turns towards you! Will you draw your sword to defend yourself (turn to 268) or cast a spell?

DUD	RAZ	ROK	ZAP	KIN
478	372	352	455	382

186

With outstanding bravery, you grit your teeth and let your blade do its work. You gasp as the task is completed and you are freed. But to what avail? You will certainly not be able to complete your mission with only one leg. You must now do everything in your power to survive on the way back to Kharé, where you may be able to find a doctor. But your mission must certainly end here . . .

187

After the battle, you decide to leave the area quickly, in case any other Snattacats visit this spot. You continue along the trail for a few minutes until you reach a suitable clearing where you can catch your breath. Turn to 20.

188

The KLATTAMEN you have encountered are a fearless, yet fool-hardy, bunch. Within their tribes, brawn is an attribute valued above brains. You draw your weapon and attack the creatures. Each is anxious to be the one who deals you the death blow; they all attack together. You must decide each Attack Round which of the Klattamen you are attacking and conduct the battle in the normal way. Roll Attack Strengths for the two remaining Klattamen. If either of them exceed your Attack Strength, then they will inflict a wound on you. Resolve this combat:

First KLATTAMAN	SKILL 8	STAMINA 7
Second KLATTAMAN	SKILL 8	STAMINA 6
Third KLATTAMAN	SKILL 7	STAMINA 7

If you defeat the Klattamen, turn to 251.

189

By using your intelligence, you begin to make some sense of the writing. Soon you have a good idea of its meaning and you read it aloud: 'This temple was built by the priests of Yadu in honour of Throff, goddess of the earth. Those who are not of the faith are forbidden from entering and shall be punished accordingly if they dare to speak the name of Throff in this temple . . .' You stop, realizing what you have done! According to this message, punishment will befall you as you have now spoken the goddess's name twice and you do not worship her as your god! All is silent. Has the goddess now left this place? A rumbling makes you fear otherwise. The ground is shaking! A cracking noise makes you look up in time to see a huge slab of marble falling directly on top of you! You leap aside just in time to avoid being crushed as the great stone smashes on the ground. But you land awkwardly, twisting your ankle – lose 2 STAMINA points. Do you want to rush for the entrance (turn to 135) or will you cast a spell?

| FOF | ROK | FIX | MAG | NEP |
| 429 | 369 | 481 | 335 | 412 |

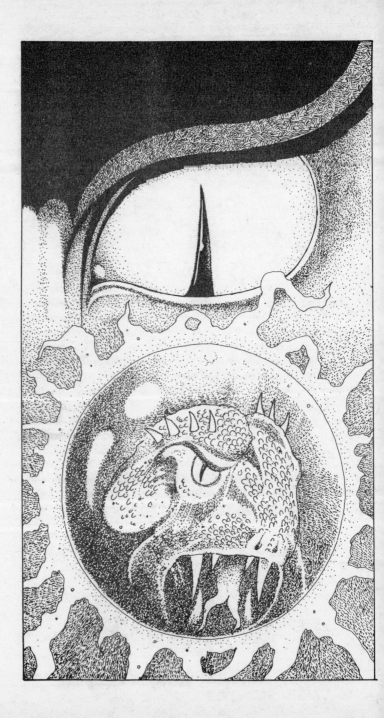

190

At the end of the passageway, a small room is lit by a single candle standing on a wooden table. The candlelight reveals a murky room, but one used as a place of residence, judging by the furniture scattered about. Seated at the table is a spindly creature whose attention is focused on a Glass Orb standing on a plinth. The creature is mumbling something at the Orb. Shapes and colours are swirling across its surface, but you cannot make out anything clearly. Will you politely disturb the creature to announce yourself (turn to **282**) or draw your weapon and attack (turn to **29**)?

191

Choose your spell quickly:

DUD	BIG	SUN	ZAP	MAG
370	440	334	488	345

If you know none of these, draw your weapon and turn to **286**.

192

A murmur spreads through the onlookers and they look towards you suspiciously. 'Perhaps our wealthy friend is not so wealthy after all,' says one of the Elves. 'Perhaps our food isn't good enough!' says another. The atmosphere is becoming decidedly hostile. Will you tell them you'd like to look around their camp first (turn to **112**) or tell them you are a trader and you wish to *trade* for their food (turn to **79**)?

193

You leave your pack and move along the tree, looking carefully for signs of whatever caused the noise. You see nothing. But a low growling sound comes from the area where you were resting. Still you see nothing. Your pack topples from the tree trunk on to the ground. Something is not quite right here. You are *certain* your pack was resting in a level position. It almost seems as though something has pushed it off. The low growling turns into a vicious roar. *Something* launches itself forward and fastens sharp teeth around your arm! You are being attacked by an invisible beast! You quickly pull out your weapon and bring it down heavily on the creature's head. It yelps and releases its grip, freeing your arm. You must lose 2 STAMINA points for this painful injury. Will you now run away from this place (turn to **271**) or do you wish to know more about your attacker (turn to **90**)?

194

As you draw your weapon, so do the Goblins. Resolve this battle:

First MARSH GOBLIN	SKILL 7	STAMINA 6
Second MARSH GOBLIN	SKILL 6	STAMINA 5
Third MARSH GOBLIN	SKILL 6	STAMINA 6
Fourth MARSH GOBLIN	SKILL 5	STAMINA 6

Fight the Goblins one at a time. If you kill all four, turn to **277**. If at any time you wish to run away from the battle, turn to **168**.

195

The lucky charm is a small golden snake which can be hung around your neck. In fact it is a particularly useful piece in that it will restore your LUCK to its *Initial* level – but once only. You may either wear it now to restore your LUCK immediately, or save it until you feel it would be more useful. But once you have used it, it will not work again, although its gold content is worth 1 Gold Piece to you. Now turn to **92** to leave the Elf's home.

196

The Hewing Axe is a magical weapon, especially effective against the man-trap plants in the Forest of the Snatta. With this axe you will free yourself easily from the STRANGLEBUSH. Turn to **106**.

197

Do you have any of the following with you:

Sand?	Turn to **148**
A tinderbox?	Turn to **266**
Borrinskin boots?	Turn to **319**

If you have none of these, you must either return to **123** to choose again, or leave the area without delay (turn to **306**).

198

The old Elf stands up to take you to the store. 'My friend,' he says, 'it is years since we have heard stories as good as those. We are indeed traders and businessfolk. But as reward for the merriment you have given us, we will offer you our *best* prices.' When you reach the goods caravan, you may buy any items for sale at half the normal price. And as a special present, the old Elf will give you one item in the store as a gift. Now turn to **315**.

199

After packing up your camp, you pull out the little whistle and blow. No sound comes from it. You shake it vigorously and blow again, but there is still no sound. But it is not broken. It emits a high-pitched whistle, silent to the ears, but which can be heard by the ferryman. A few minutes later, he comes stumbling out of the undergrowth. 'All right, all right. Hold yer horses. I'm coming. Wot's yer rush?' He is a scruffy, unwashed individual, somewhat overweight but with a broad pair of shoulders. 'Right then,' he says, scratching himself across the chest, 'where to?' You tell him you wish to cross the lake, whereupon he bursts into laughter, slapping his knees with his hands. 'Of course yer wants to cross the lake!' he laughs. '*Everyone* wants to cross the lake. But I still asks "Where to" anyway. Just my little jest. Right then. That'll be 4 Gold Pieces. In advance, if yer don't mind.' Will you pay the man his fee (turn to **110**) or, if you haven't that much money, try to fight or trick him (turn to **49**)?

200

The man puts down his pipe. 'Sshhh. *Ssssss*, my slithery sistersss. Soundsss like someone'sss calling usss.' He looks up to see you and waves you down. 'A visitor! Join uss, stranger.' Will you climb down into the pit (turn to **301**) or would you prefer to leave this man to his snakes (turn to **318**)?

201

Your constitution is low and your foolhardy refusal to shelter from the storm was not a wise move. You begin to sneeze. Unless you receive proper treatment within the next few days, the pneumonia you have caught will seriously affect you. Tomorrow morning, the disease will have taken a grip and you must deduct 2 SKILL and 2 STAMINA points. Thereafter, every morning you must deduct another 1 SKILL point and 3 STAMINA points unless you are able to rid yourself of the disease. Nevertheless, you soldier on through the storm until it eventually subsides. Turn to **10**.

202

One by one, the snakes dart at you, biting with their fangs. Fight them in sequence:

First SNAKE	SKILL 7	STAMINA 3
Second SNAKE	SKILL 6	STAMINA 1
Third SNAKE	SKILL 6	STAMINA 4
Fourth SNAKE	SKILL 5	STAMINA 2
Fifth SNAKE	SKILL 6	STAMINA 2
Sixth SNAKE	SKILL 7	STAMINA 1

If you defeat all the snakes, you may turn to the Snake Charmer:

SNAKE CHARMER	SKILL 6	STAMINA 7

If you do not defeat the Snake Charmer within five Attack Rounds, turn to **312**. If you do, turn to **260**.

203

The parchment is worn and faded. A heading at the top reads 'Secrets of the Baklands', although most of the writing is illegible. By studying it carefully, you can just about make out two facts which may be useful. An old sorceress known as 'The Sham' may be worth visiting, as her powers and knowledge are considerable and she is not wholly aligned to the dark side of sorcery. She dwells ahead on the Klatta-Bak Steppes in an area that must be north-east of where you are now. She appreciates being given gifts, but the parchment gives a warning: she is not what she appears to be. Secondly, the parchment warns of the Forest of the Snatta. In this forest the plants are as deadly as the animals. But the most deadly of the plants are affected by Essence of Bark. The rest of the parchment cannot be deciphered. Turn to **86**.

204

You follow them to the fire where they offer you meat from the roasting animal, apparently some kind of wild boar. You may add 2 STAMINA points for this meal (1 only if you have already eaten). You try in vain to communicate with them, but their language is very basic, if indeed they have a language at all. They offer also a mug of tea-like broth to wash down your food. You are beginning to wonder what on earth they want with you if you cannot even speak to each other, when a sound behind you, followed by a hushed silence from the crowd, gives you your answer. You turn to see a well-built Klattaman, taller and stronger than the rest, standing behind you. He looks at you and curls his lips into a low growl. In his hand he holds a club which he picks up and grips firmly. You rise to your feet and face this champion. A fight has been planned for you. Will you use your magic against this foe (turn to **229**) or draw your weapon (turn to **280**)?

205

The wounded creature steps back, clutching its arm. The shimmering haze returns once more to engulf the Deathwraith. It rises into the air and, as it does so, the apparition has disappeared. In its place stands a stout, balding man who whimpers and nurses his wounds. 'Enough!' he cries. 'Let me be! I did you no harm. Why do you attack me?' Your jaw drops at the sight. 'Leave Renfren alone. He never does any harm. Just a little merriment, that's all.' You are not amused at the man's practical jokes. Do you want to step in and finish him off (turn to **326**) or will you threaten him unless he gives you information (turn to **72**)?

206

You fall on your knees and pray for mercy, hoping the goddess will take pity on you. The rumblings subside and the dust begins to settle. Is she allowing you to take your freedom? In front of you, one of the wall-mounted statues starts to speak. It is a woman in leather armour with a bronze helmet – evidently a likeness of the goddess. Its words reach you: 'Mortal, you are not of my faith. Yet you invade my holy temple and then beg me for mercy. But I am a just god. I will allow you to escape with your life, on one condition. You must renounce Libra, your own goddess, and from now on worship Throff. Do this and I shall grant you your freedom. Otherwise you shall perish. The choice is yours.'

What will your answer be? Will you accept and worship Throff (if you do this you may never again call on Libra's help at any stage of your quest) to escape with your life (turn to **298**), or will you resist and take your chances with her wrath (turn to **238**)?

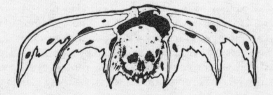

207

You draw your weapon and march forward with resolve. You aim to break their circle. As you step forward, the voice comes again: 'Stop, foolish creature. This warning shall be your last. As shall be your next step if you heed not my warning!' Will you ignore this warning and continue (turn to **140**) or do you think you had better stop (turn to **232**)?

208

You try a few words of greeting, but they seem not to understand you at all. Then they speak to you, but you can make no sense of their language, if you do not know an interpretation spell. Return to **316** and choose again.

209

'So *you* have the Serpent Ring, Analander!' the Air Serpent hisses. 'If such be the case, I am bound by its power to aid you with advice. But even the Serpent Ring will not protect you from my wrath! Very well: in the dark chamber of night, do not light your way with the blood candle. Such is my advice. But it will be of no use to you, for these next few moments will be your last on this earth!' Now return to **223** and choose your next course of action.

210

'So it's "foe", is it?' says the squeaky voice, before you have had a chance to open your mouth. 'Then do as I say. Get out of my way!' Will you stand aside and let the little fellow pass (turn to **114**) or do you resent being ordered about like this (turn to **181**)?

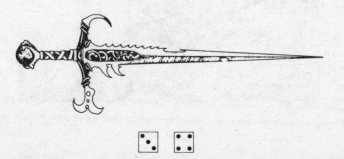

211

Roll two dice and compare the total with your SKILL. If the roll is lower than your SKILL, you manage to grab the edge and can begin pulling yourself out of the pit. Whatever it was on the rim of the pit will still be there, but if it bites you, you may this time bear with the pain until you reach the top. *Test your Luck*. If you are *Lucky*, the creature bites only one hand (1 STAMINA point of damage). If you are *Unlucky*, it bites both (2 STAMINA points of damage). Eventually you climb up on to the surface. Turn to **43**.

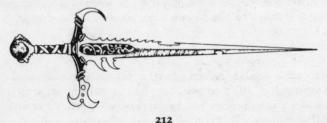

212

You pull out your vial of Bark Essence and take the stopper off. The branches react immediately, releasing their grip on you. You pour a little Essence on to your hands and rub it in. Seconds later, the bush has freed you completely. It seems that this STRANGLEBUSH attacks animals only. With the Bark Essence, it has mistaken you for a plant! Turn to **106**.

213

Having rid yourself of the Air Serpent, you set off. You take the oars of the boat and row yourself across the great lake. The going is not easy as the water is thick and heavy. In the centre of the lake you stop. Several yards ahead of you the water is bubbling up. Do you wish to see what this bubbling is (turn to **28**) or will you steer a wide course around to avoid it (turn to **36**)?

214

The trail leads onwards to a point where a tall tree has fallen across the way just at the point where another path joins your own. You stop at the tree to rest. You may take Provisions here and you can add 2 STAMINA points if this is your first meal of the day. While you are sitting on the trunk, the forest noises keep you alert. Small animals rustle in the undergrowth, birds call; but one particular sound puts you on your guard. A soft plop, which seems to come from the tree trunk, cannot be matched to anything happening around you. Do you wish to investigate the sound (turn to **193**) or will you instead continue onwards (turn to **120**)?

215

Eyebrows rise and the Elves look at one another at the thought that you may be carrying Gold. 'Our pardon, noble traveller,' says the old Elf. 'We mistook you for a vagabond. We are always happy to offer our hospitality to those who can afford the price. Such is our business. Come, let me show you to the kitchen tent where you may eat and we may exchange news of the outside world. It is just beyond that caravan over there.' You follow him across the camp, with the rest of the Elves following several paces behind and muttering to themselves. Do you want to go to the kitchen tent (turn to **321**) or are you already thinking about escaping from here (turn to **311**)?

216

As your blow strikes the creature, a short jet of liquid spits from its mouth and lands on your leg. A burning sensation warns you: the Beetle's spit is an acidic liquid which will certainly eat flesh. Deduct 1 STAMINA point for the burn on your leg. Continue your fight, but each time you hit the Beetle, roll one die to see whether its acid spit hits you:

Roll	Effect
1	Hits you in the face. Lose 3 STAMINA points and the sight of your left eye.
2	Hits your sword arm. Lose 2 STAMINA points and 1 SKILL point.
3	Hits your other arm. Lose 2 STAMINA points.
4	Hits your leg. Lose 1 STAMINA point.
5–6	Misses.

If you defeat the creature, turn to **24**.

217

The going becomes more tiring in the late morning. You are walking up an incline which forms the natural boundary between the plains of Baddu-Bak and the Klatta-Bak Steppes. As the ground levels out once more you can see something in the distance ahead of you. Perhaps man-made or perhaps a freak of nature, this actually looks like a construction of some kind. As you get closer you can see more clearly what it is – or rather, what it *was*. A ruined building stands on a stone plinth, its columns cracked and broken. The elaborate carvings on the pillars suggest it was perhaps a temple of some kind, sited by a natural well which has now dried up. Do you want to investigate these ruins (turn to **63**), check the well (turn to **23**) or leave (turn to **309**)?

218

You land in the pit screaming loudly to frighten the Snake Charmer. But instead of being frightened, his tune becomes faster. You are horrified as the snakes dart towards you, hissing menacingly. Turn to **202**.

219

The dust storm rages around you and you dare not look out to see what is happening. For half an hour you sit and wait until finally the winds calm and the storm moves on. Turn to **10**.

220

As the Serpent's power dies, so does the living earth. Everything is now still. You may rest for a short while to catch your breath, then set off again towards the forest. Turn to **165**.

221

This whistle summons the ferryman of Lake Ilklala. Fenestra tells you how it works: 'The ferryman patrols the lake shore every morning and you will attract his attention by blowing this whistle.' First thing in the morning you may blow this whistle by turning to reference **199** if you are on the shores of Lake Ilklala. You thank Fenestra for the whistle and leave her home to rejoin the path. Turn to **92**. You may add 3 LUCK points for finding this whistle.

222

The Rock Demon crashes to the ground. But the battle has been watched by the cowled spectre. Will you now advance towards this creature (turn to 104) or escape from this place (turn to 113)?

223

With your hand on your weapon, you order the ferryman to take the oars himself; you are not going to row his boat. You turn angrily towards him but stop in mid-sentence as you see a transformation taking place. Before your eyes, the ferryman is shrivelling as if the air were being let out of a balloon! From his collapsing form, a jet of gas rises into the air, swirling round and forming the shape of a winged serpent! Will you draw out your weapon (turn to 261) or cast a spell?

ZAP	KIN	SIX	DUM	HUF
363	419	482	464	350

Or will you instead investigate the body of the ferryman (turn to 21)?

224

You spend a miserable night, unsheltered and on your guard against attack. Nevertheless, you manage to get some sleep and you rise at dawn. Gain 2 STAMINA points for your rest. Did you eat at all yesterday? If not, deduct 3 STAMINA points as you are now very hungry. You may continue your journey by heading either to the north-east (turn to 15) or to the north-west (turn to 217).

225

You settle down and make camp for the night. If you have Provisions you may eat and if you do so you can add 2 STAMINA points if this is your first meal of the day or 1 STAMINA point if you have already eaten. You cover yourself and curl up on the ground to sleep; it has been a tiring day. Ten minutes later you are fast asleep.

Suddenly you are startled and spring to your feet! A hissing coil of fire hovers above you in the air! Two sharp talons reach down and grab at your pack. The Serpent of Fire clutches your rucksack and beats its wings to lift it into the air. Will you dive on to your pack and hold on for dear life (turn to 100) or allow the Serpent to fly off with it, but follow along on foot (turn to 58)?

226

You step into the undergrowth and climb forward into the bushes. A flash of red ahead reassures you that you are heading in the right direction. But the snake seems to be moving a little slower than it could – almost as if it *wants* you to follow it. It stops at the foot of a tree and coils round the trunk. You watch as it slithers up the trunk into the branches. Its head drops down from the foliage to look for you. Do you walk up to the tree, ready for danger (turn to **123**), or are you convinced that there is nothing particularly interesting about this snake so you may as well head back to the path (turn to **306**)?

227

The Hewing Axe has a magical blade and will cut down trees with one blow. It may be used in battle, but if you use it as a weapon, you must deduct 2 points from your Attack Strength roll. Now turn to **86**.

228

'The bootsss!' he hisses. 'Give, give, give.' You hand them to him and he is silent. He looks slyly at you, but then agrees to keep his part of the bargain. You ask whether his snakes are anything to do with the Seven Serpents, but he shakes his head. 'Nooo, thesse are my sissterss. But the Seven Sserpentss passsed over two dayss ago. My sissterss know their plansss.' He can tell you the whereabouts of one of the Serpents. Do you wish to leave, following his directions (turn to **12**)? Otherwise you may climb out of the pit and continue in the direction you were going (turn to **318**).

229

Which spell will you use?

SAP	RES	DUD	GAK	LAW
340	402	494	420	457

If you know none of these, you will have to use your weapon. Turn to **280**.

230

You carry on along the trail and stop suddenly as you notice a movement in the distance to the west. Three shapes are moving rapidly across the plain throwing up a thick cloud of dust. They turn and head towards you. As there is no cover, you have no choice but to let them approach. They come closer and you can make out three riders on horseback. But as they draw near, you realize that the riders you saw were not riders at all: three Centaurs are approaching. You must think quickly how you will greet them. Will you be friendly (turn to 111) or adopt an aggressive approach (turn to 313)?

231

After the soup, a plate of bread and runny cheese is brought to you. The smell is awful! But with all eyes on you, you force down the stuff and wash the taste away with your herb tea. Gloister is a strange, cheese-like substance, which has the power to restore LUCK. You may restore your LUCK to its *Initial* level. You may also add 2 STAMINA points if this is your first meal today (1 STAMINA point if you have already eaten). The old Elf orders another cup of herb tea and the two of you chat, with the others looking on. Will you:

Try to amuse them by telling them jokes?	Turn to 275
Tell them you are tired and would like to rest for the night?	Turn to 69
Ask to see their wares if, as they appear, they are traders?	Turn to 315

232

'A wise move, mortal; a very wise move.' The spirit's voice calms down. Now you must decide whether to demand that they reveal their magical chant (turn to 166) or ask them for some proof of their identities (turn to 323.)

233

For an hour, you wait. But apart from the occasional small animal which scurries out of the forest to take a drink, the area seems to be completely deserted. Would you like to wander along the shore to see whether you can find anyone (turn to 241), call out for help (turn to 57), or will you wait a little longer (turn to 304)?

234

'So you also use the mystic arts!' she exclaims. 'Then we certainly do have much in common.' You chat to her for some time, comparing spell notes. She has a good supply of spell artefacts and she will exchange these with you. You must give her two items which are used in your spells and will receive in return *one* spell artefact of your choice (she has all the items needed for the spells in the Spell Book). She is delighted to have found someone of similar profession. Turn to **183**.

235

You spend an undisturbed night on the fringe of the forest. You may add 3 STAMINA points for your night's rest. But if you did not eat at all yesterday, you must deduct 3 STAMINA points. Three paths now lead into the depths of the forest. Which will you choose?

The left-hand path?	Turn to **13**
The right-hand path?	Turn to **329**
The middle path?	Turn to **214**

236

The heat increases as more of the glowing rocks break through the surface. You are drenched in sweat and must deduct 1 STAMINA point for the pain. You had better now try to climb out of the pit. Turn to **211**.

237

You set up your camp. You may eat Provisions if you wish before you sleep. Gain 2 STAMINA points if this is your first meal today, or 1 STAMINA point if you have already eaten. You lie down to sleep for the night. Noises wake you continually during the night, but you get some sleep and rise at dawn to continue. Add 1 STAMINA point for your rest, but deduct 3 STAMINA points if you did not eat yesterday. Turn to 11.

238

You refuse her offer. The statue's expression turns to one of anger. 'Very well then, fool. If that is your choice, so be it!' Again the rumblings start, but this time with renewed vigour. A pillar falls on your leg, crushing it painfully. But your agony is shortlived as a slab of stone drops from the ceiling on to your chest. Your adventure has ended here in the Temple of Throff.

239

You can head out to the north-west (turn to 149) or you can take a wide detour around the creature and then continue northwards (turn to 283).

240

As you step away from their slain champion, you can feel the atmosphere in the crowd has changed. One of the creatures steps forward with another joint of meat from the roast for you to chew. But you have decided it wisest to leave the village as quickly as possible. You turn and walk away from the crowd towards the far side of their village. Turn to **173**.

241

For half an hour you follow the shore westwards, but find nothing. You walk back and try the other way. Again you come across nothing that might help you get across. Do you wish to shout out in the hope of attracting someone's attention (turn to **57**) or sit and wait to see whether any help might arrive (turn to **233**)?

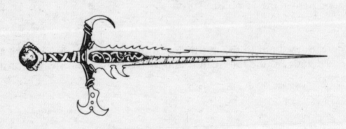

242

Your hand reaches down to pull out your weapon. As you touch it, a jolt passes up your arm, causing you to pull away quickly! You shake your arm painfully. Lose 1 STAMINA point. Cautiously, you reach down to try again. As soon as your hand touches the weapon, the same painful spasm shoots up your arm. Lose another STAMINA point. Something magical is preventing you from drawing your weapon! Will you carry on regardless (turn to **190**) or would you prefer to turn round, leave this place and continue along the trail (turn to **92**)?

243

You pray desperately to Libra for help and wait for a sign that the goddess has heard your plea. But no such sign comes and the aching in your limbs becomes almost unbearable. Carrion crows circle above you, squawking loudly and waiting to enjoy their next meal. One of them lands on the cross and pecks at your wrist. You are powerless to prevent it but you shout to frighten it off. It soon alights again and once more pecks at your wrist. You must lose 3 STAMINA points, for your strength is fading. The crow pecks again. But this time you do not shout. Your head turns towards the scrawny creature and a weak smile spreads across your lips. It seems not to be attempting to eat you, but instead to peck through your binding! Libra has not forsaken you! Moments later, your hand is free, allowing you to hold on while the bird pecks at your other ties. Soon you are released and the crow caws as it springs from the cross and flies up into the sky. With your last reserves of strength, you slide down the pole and rest, panting, at the base. But your ordeal has cost you dearly. Although the Black Elves have left your weapon and backpack at the base of the cross, they have taken all your other possessions. And you have called on Libra's help. You may not pray to her again in the Baklands. Nevertheless, you must continue your journey. Turn to **269**.

244

Further along the trail you come across a clearing where you can rest. If you wish to eat Provisions here you may do so and add 2 STAMINA points (1 STAMINA point if you have already eaten today). As you stand to leave, a cracking sound makes you turn quickly. Breaking through the undergrowth towards you is a tall, lumbering WILD BEAR! The creature bars your way forward and you will have to fight it. Will you draw your weapon (turn to **139**) or cast a spell?

LAW	SIX	YAP	DUM	FIX
437	415	361	485	333

245

What will you find to use in your backpack?

A flask of oil?	Turn to **14**
A lucky talisman?	Turn to **278**
Snake-bite antidote?	Turn to **81**

If you have none of these, you must return to **303** and make another choice.

246

You stand up and turn to run. But before you have taken a step, you howl in pain as something digs into your leg. Of course! The invisible something that tripped you up! It must have been a Snattacat drinking from the stream. Its sharp teeth will cause 2 STAMINA points of damage. Quickly, you strike out with your weapon at where you assume its head should be. The creature yelps and releases its grip. Your blow has also broken its concentration; the Snattacat materializes in front of you. You will have to fight it quickly before the others arrive:

SNATTACAT   SKILL 7   STAMINA 9

The Snattacat has the ability to make itself invisible, which it will always do in a battle. While it is invisible, you must deduct 2 points from your Attack Strength rolls as it is difficult to fight. However, each time you wound it, you will break its concentration and it will become visible for the next Attack Round. When it is visible, attack it as normal. If you defeat the Snattacat within 6 Attack Rounds, turn to **41**. If you do not defeat it in this time, the other Snattacats will join in – turn to **99**.

247

Turning up the collar on your tunic, you set off towards the horizon. The wind swells and forceful gusts blow you roughly from one side to the other. Then it happens – the skies open up. A torrential downpour bursts from the clouds and in an instant you are soaked to the skin. Unsheltered from the wind and the rain, you have two concerns: firstly, anything you have in your backpack which would be destroyed by water *is* destroyed (maps, parchments, etc. – but not Provisions); secondly, you risk catching pneumonia as you continue through the biting wind, soaked to the skin. Roll three dice and compare the total with your STAMINA score. If the total rolled is less than your STAMINA, turn to **284**. If the total rolled is equal to or greater than your STAMINA, turn to **201**.

248

As the notes come from his pipe, your anxiety subsides. The tune is soft and peaceful and you become transfixed watching him play. His gentle music is soothing you to sleep! You realize you are falling under his hypnotic power. You settle down on the ground and, as you do so, the tune becomes a series of shrill whistles. Your hands are changing. Scales are appearing on your fingers! You rub your face and it is tough and leathery. A smile spreads across his lips as he gloats over his latest victim. You are destined to spend the rest of your life as one of the Snake Charmer's pets . . .

249

The Earth Serpent spies the ring. 'Enemy of Mampang!' it hisses at you. 'You have found the Serpent Ring! Then, as our gods decree, I must tell you this: offer no gold to Valignya if you value your life! But this knowledge will do you no good. Here is another offering!' The Serpent darts out at you and narrowly misses striking your arm. Now return to **263** to deal with the Serpent.

250

You struggle with the hieroglyphics, but it is no use. You can make no sense of them. Frustrated and angry, you may now either open the trapdoor (turn to **180**), keep searching around the ruins (turn to **101**) or go outside to investigate the well (turn to **23**).

251

Looking through the Klattamen's things you find nothing particularly exciting. One has a couple of Gold Pieces and the spine of a rat. Another has a pouch containing a weight of sand, which is tied to the end of a stick. Perhaps this is a weapon of some kind. The amulet hanging around the neck of the third must have been a prized possession. Set in the centre of the amulet is a glowing stone – a Sun Jewel – which gives off its own natural light. You may take any three of these.

Add 1 STAMINA point for this night's rest as your sleep was interrupted. And if you ate nothing yesterday, deduct 3 STAMINA points for your hunger. Now you must decide which direction to continue in. Will you head north-west (turn to **83**), north-north-west (turn to **283**) or straight ahead northwards (turn to **60**)?

252

'Fool!' she scoffs. 'Do you think I will help a stranger who was ready to hold a weapon against me? Take your leave. And quickly, for that jolt you felt was only a sample of my power.' Her gaze is fixed on you and her wide eyes light up, glowing like coals. You decide not to risk tangling with her and head back for the door. Outside you rejoin the path and continue on your way. Turn to **92**.

253

Giant leeches live in the swamps and you pick up three as you wade through the water. These will cause you 2 STAMINA points of damage, feasting on your blood, unless you have a tinderbox which you can use to burn them off before they are able to bite. Turn next to **182**.

254

You run along after it, fumbling with your possessions for something else to give. Choose something else – again, this must be something valuable, not worthless – and return to **50** to find out its reaction. But your generosity in offering *two* gifts is appreciated. Add 2 to the die roll.

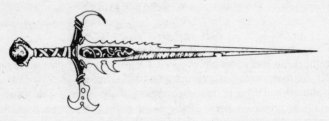

255

You continue walking north through the night. You may stop along the way to eat Provisions. If you wish to do this, you can add 2 STAMINA points if this is your first meal of the day, or 1 if you have already eaten. But going without sleep will make you tired – deduct 2 STAMINA points. And if you did not eat at all during the day, you must deduct another 3 STAMINA points for your hunger. But you make good progress and encounter nothing. At dawn you are walking uphill as you enter the Klatta-Bak Steppes. From a vantage point you can survey the bleak countryside, but there are no features to guide you. Will you travel north-westwards (turn to **83**), north-north-westwards (turn to **283**) or continue northwards (turn to **60**)?

256

The fox snarls at you as you stand up, weapon at the ready. It is hungry and will kill to satisfy its appetite. Its fiery red fur bristles along its back. Resolve your fight with the creature:

FIREFOX   SKILL 7   STAMINA 6

When you have inflicted your first wound on the creature, turn to 71.

257

The leader motions for the others to be silent. 'Quiet, pighead,' he orders. 'No one would be so foolish as to cross these plains alone if they were not protected in some way. Are you a sorcerer, friend?' You tell him you are, and offer to cast a Luck Spell over them if they will aid you. At this promise, they become quite excited, stomping their hooves on the ground and smiling at you. 'You have yourself a bargain,' says the leader. 'How may we be of service?' You ask them to help you on your way. 'We can take you a little further across the plains if you wish. But it is a long journey to any civilized place. To the north-west lives Manata, the Snake Charmer, and to the north-east, we may still find a caravan heading towards Kharé. We can take you to either of these. But first, our reward!' You mumble a few words and wave your fingers at them, telling them they are now blessed with luck. Horsemen are not the brightest of creatures, and they look at each other proudly. Where will you now have them take you? To the north-west (turn to 64) or to the north-east (turn to 2)?

258

You draw your weapon and wait for the creatures to attack. They circle quickly, picking up pace, until finally they dart down towards you in an attacking line. Their speed makes them difficult targets. Choose which you will fight and roll for Attack Strength. Roll also for the Attack Strengths of the Nighthawks. If your Attack Strength is higher than that of your target, you have wounded it, but each Nighthawk rolling a higher Attack Strength than you will wound you. Resolve your combat:

First NIGHTHAWK   SKILL 7   STAMINA 5
Second NIGHTHAWK   SKILL 6   STAMINA 5
Third NIGHTHAWK   SKILL 7   STAMINA 5
Fourth NIGHTHAWK   SKILL 7   STAMINA 4

After three Attack Rounds, turn to 314.

259

You hold your arms up in the air and walk slowly forward. To your relief, no more arrows are released, although you can see bowmen, with shafts at the ready, covering your approach. A crowd is gathering to see who you are and you are soon close enough to make out what sort of people are watching you. You have come across a caravan of Black Elves, presumably traders of some kind. As you enter the camp, they eye you suspiciously. An old Elf, slightly stouter than the rest, steps forward. 'If you seek shelter or food,' he starts, 'then you waste your time with this caravan. What purpose have you wandering alone through the Baklands?' What will your reply be?

Will you claim to be a trader and ask to see their wares?	Turn to **315**
Will you tell him of your mission and ask about the Seven Serpents?	Turn to **37**
Will you tell him you *are* after food and shelter and that you will pay handsomely for their hospitality?	Turn to **215**

260

You search the pit, looking for any valuable possessions the Snake Charmer may have hidden. You find his Bamboo Pipe and, in a sack which was partly covered with earth, you find a bottle of Holy Water. You may keep these. Now you must set off on your journey once more. But were you bitten by any of the snakes while you were in the pit? Each of the snakes was poisonous. If any of them wounded you, the slow-acting poison will take effect. If you already have snake-bite antidote, you may take this to neutralize the poison. If you do not have this, you will die unless you can find some by the end of the day. The poison will weaken you such that any STAMINA penalties you take between now and dusk will inflict double damage (i.e. you will subtract double the STAMINA penalties). Leave the snake pit and continue your journey – turn to **318**.

261

The creature facing you is the AIR SERPENT, who is a dangerous foe. Your blows will not harm it, as it is made of the air itself; but should you catch it twice in succession, you will disperse part of its body, making it difficult for it to re-form. The Serpent will attack you by trying to engulf your head with its body, thus making you breathe in its choking gas. Resolve the fight:

AIR SERPENT   SKILL 11   STAMINA 14

You will only harm the Air Serpent if you roll a higher Attack Strength twice in succession, in which case you can deduct 3 STAMINA points from the Serpent after this second attack. The Serpent's gas will only do 1 STAMINA point of damage to you, unless the Serpent rolls a higher Attack Strength twice (or more) in succession. In this case, the effects of the gas are multiplied: 1 STAMINA penalty in the first round, 2 STAMINA penalties in the second, 4 in the third, 8 in the fourth, etc. If you defeat the creature, turn to **213**.

262

On your way out of the ruined temple, you may investigate the well (turn to **23**); otherwise turn to **309** to leave the area.

263

You reach down to grab the creature. It darts at you to bite your hand, but you manage to swat it to the ground. Only then do you see the snake as it really is . . .

As it lies on the ground, its skin splits. From within, a dark brown serpent emerges. As if in some sort of reaction to its exposure to the air, the Earth Serpent grows rapidly before your eyes! It unfurls great wings and coils up before you, hissing menacingly. How will you fight it? With a spell?

DUM	HUF	DOZ	NAP	ZEN
367	351	491	443	471

With your weapon (turn to **54**)? Or with your bare hands (turn to **66**)?

264

You awake early the next morning. If you did not eat at all yesterday, you must deduct 3 STAMINA points for your lack of food. What have you decided to do about getting across the lake? Will you follow the shoreline looking for signs of life (turn to 241), call out to see whether you can attract someone's attention (turn to 57) or wait to see whether any help might arrive (turn to 233)?

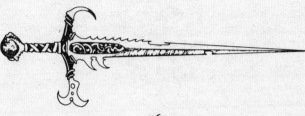

265

The door opens to allow you into a dark passageway. Following the passage downwards, you can eventually see a glowing light ahead of you. And you can hear voices. Will you creep along to the end to see what is happening (turn to 190) or draw your weapon and march on boldly (turn to 242)?

266

You pull out your tinderbox and try to make a fire. The Serpent watches you from the tree above, almost bemusedly. It is interested in your plan. But unfortunately this plan will have no effect against the Fire Serpent you face. The Serpent drops from the branches on top of you and you must fight it:

FIRE SERPENT   SKILL 13   STAMINA 12

If you defeat it, turn to 306.

267

You call out to the whirlwind. Although it gives a little 'kick' in the air, you cannot be certain whether this is a reaction to your voice or merely a chance movement. You call again: no reaction. Will you now approach it to investigate more closely (turn to 157) or leave (turn to 322)?

268

The battle commences:

ROCK DEMON   SKILL 10   STAMINA 12

You are still caught in the folds of the rock and must deduct 2 points from your Attack Strength dice roll until you free yourself. You will be able to free yourself if you can roll a number on two dice which is less than your SKILL. But each attempt to free yourself leaves you open to attack by the Rock Demon for an automatic wound of 2 STAMINA points. If you defeat the creature, turn to 222.

269

Night is soon upon you. You must shortly choose either to bed down for the night or continue through the night across the Baklands. If you wish to rest, turn to 237; if you will continue, turn to 144.

270

You quickly collect your things together and make off through the reeds away from whatever it is that approaches. Soon the noise is well behind you. Without leaving the swamp, you continue under cover of the vegetation. Turn to **295**.

271

Leaving the fallen tree behind, you continue through the woods until you reach a fork in the path. Will you follow the path to the left (turn to **119**) or to the right (turn to **329**)?

272

Are you able to read the hieroglyphics? If you are lucky there will be similarities between its language and other ancient languages you have studied. *Test your Luck*, if you wish to try reading them. If you are *Lucky*, turn to **189**. If you are *Unlucky*, turn to **250**. You may cast a spell if you wish, either before or after you *Test your Luck*, but before you turn to the next reference:

POP	WAL	GUM	SUS	DOC
489	417	374	401	465

If you do not wish to use your LUCK here, turn to **101** and make another choice.

273

A long trek now lies ahead of you across the Baddu-Bak Plains. In which direction will you head? To the north-west (turn to **176**), north-north-east (turn to **137**) or north-east (turn to **85**)?

274

The trail leads through the woods. You follow it for a couple of hours. The path is downhill and you make good progress. You are walking alongside a stream when suddenly, for no apparent reason, you trip over. You feel that you have kicked something close to the water, but there is nothing there! You sit up and look around. You are horrified to see four dark pairs of eyes staring at you from behind a bush. The eyes move forward and you can see the creatures watching you. SNATTACATS! They are about the size of large dogs, with ugly snub noses. Their black fur is trimmed with yellow flashes. They step towards you – and disappear! You blink and look again, but they are nowhere to be seen. You listen carefully. Their footsteps cannot be disguised: they are advancing towards you. Will you spring to your feet and run off ahead down the path (turn to **246**), stand and face them with your weapon (turn to **99**) or cast a spell?

FAR	FOF	ROK	GUM	GOB
467	**454**	**431**	**376**	**343**

275

You hope that a couple of jokes will make them less hostile towards you. Your favourite jokes are Goblin jokes, as Goblins are well-known for their stupidity. You ask the old Elf why the Goblin wedding cake was made out of Skunkbear dung. He shrugs. You tell him: *to keep the flies off the bride!* The tent bursts into uproarious laughter, and the old Elf, with tears streaming from his eyes, claps you on the back. You tell them the one about the Goblin who never learned to spell his own name – because he thought only wizards could *spell*! Again, laughter resounds around the tent. You are the star of the show and the Elves' mischievous looks have now turned to friendly smiles. What do you wish to do next? You may either ask to visit their store to see whether they have anything of value to buy or trade for (turn to **198**) or ask for a place to rest for the night (turn to **26**).

276

The temperature becomes uncomfortable and beads of sweat appear on your forehead. The ground to your right breaks and another glowing rock emerges; then another to your left. You are now streaming with sweat and the heat is painful. Deduct 2 STAMINA points for your ordeal. Now you must decide whether to risk climbing out of the pit (turn to 211) or cast a spell:

BAG	MUD	FOF	DOC	FIX
418	371	486	348	406

277

Searching through the bodies, you find 6 Gold Pieces, a parchment scroll which you cannot understand, and enough nuts and berries for two meals. Then a noise startles you, coming from the same direction the Goblins were running from. Turn to 270. If you are playing as a warrior and have used no spells in this adventure, turn first to 330.

278

You hang the lucky talisman around your neck and prepare to fight the creature. Turn to 67.

279

'So *you* have the Serpent Ring, Analander!' the Serpent hisses. 'If such be the case, I am bound by its power to aid you with advice. But even the Serpent Ring will not protect you from my wrath! Very well: in the dark chamber of night, do not light your way with the blood candle. Such is my advice. But it will be of no use to you, for these next moments shall be your last on this earth!' Now return to 293 and choose your next course of action.

280

A general hubbub spreads through the crowd. They are getting excited at the thought of watching such a contest. Let the fight commence:

KLATTAMAN CHAMPION SKILL 9   STAMINA 8

If you win, turn to 240.

281

Over the side of the boat you fall, plunging down into the murky waters. You fight desperately to swim to the surface but, to your horror, something has hold of your leg and is pulling you downwards! Your lungs are bursting, but still the grip holds you under the surface. Your struggles are to no avail. Eventually you are unable to control yourself and a gasp fills your lungs with water. The unknown dangers of Lake Ilklala have claimed another victim.

282

You are about to open your mouth to greet the creature when a squeaky voice breaks the silence. 'All right, all right,' it says. 'Don't stand there stammering like a Half-Orc with the jitters. Come in and sit yourself down. I'm busy, but I'll be with you in a minute.' The voice is female; perhaps this woman is an Elf of some kind. She is engrossed in her Glass Orb, but in a few minutes she sits back and looks at you. 'So – a visitor. And a human too. I am Fenestra, Elf Sorceress. Now, I have an excuse for being here. This is my home. But you must be a long way from your home. What in Gredd's name are you doing in this forest?' She watches you intently as you explain your story, while being careful to leave out your true mission. Her eyes are too large for her face and they seem to glow softly of their own accord. The whole effect is quite disturbing. But she listens attentively and appears genuinely interested in your travels. You may ask her a question now. Will you ask her whether she has any magic which might be of use to you (turn to **234**), ask her how you may best cross Lake Ilklala (turn to **132**), or make some comment about 'strange happenings' to see whether you can steer the conversation towards the subject of the Seven Serpents (turn to **5**)?

283

Your long walk across the Baklands is coming to an end. In the distance you can see the wide fringe ahead of you that marks the boundary of the Forest of the Snatta. You climb up on to a rock to get a better view of what lies ahead. The green spread of the forest continues to the shores of Lake Ilklala, which you can just make out on the horizon. The rock you are standing on is a suitable place to eat Provisions. If you wish to do so, turn to **78**. If you do not wish to eat Provisions, turn to **300**.

284

Luckily, your constitution is good. You will catch a mild cold but otherwise your health is unaffected. Deduct 1 STAMINA point for the rest of the day (add it back on tomorrow morning). Bravely you stride on through the storm until, at last, it subsides. Turn to **10**.

285

You may head onwards either due north (turn to **170**) or north-westwards. If you choose the latter direction, you will walk for several hours until a sight makes you stop (turn to **137**).

286

The two of you close in for battle:

BADDU-BEETLE   SKILL 7   STAMINA 9

After your first hit on the creature, turn to **216**.

287

You open your eyes and shake your head. Where are you? You are lying on the ground next to your backpack, with your tunic pulled up over you. What of the sandstorm? And the Fire Serpent? Everything is as it was when you went to sleep. Was it all just a bad dream? Then, if so, why does your head ache as if it had been pounded by a mallet? You look around – and leap from your position with a cry, just as a wooden club crashes down where your head has been! Three tall, spindly creatures with powerful arms and ugly faces are staring at you. They are dressed in animal skins and carry clubs as weapons. One has an amulet around his neck. Will you draw your weapon to fight them (turn to **188**), try to talk to them (turn to **38**) or cast a spell?

YOB	KID	GAK	KIN	GOD
475	439	456	344	356

288

The old Elf becomes angry. 'The miserable Horntoad has nothing to offer!' he rages. 'But we will at least have some fun, won't we, friends?' He snaps his fingers and five burly Black Elves grab you. Holding tightly, they bundle you outside. 'Let's make an example of this wretch! A monument to the Caravan of Cesstar!' Three Elves disappear and return with two wooden poles. Fixing them together in a cross, they tie a black flag on top and fasten you securely to it by your wrists and ankles. They fix it into the ground, leaving you hanging painfully from the top. The pain causes you 4 STAMINA points of damage. An hour later, the caravan packs up camp and moves off, leaving you to the crows and the vultures. When they have gone, you may either wait to see what fate has in store (turn to **102**) or, if you are able, call on your goddess for help (turn to **243**).

289

'The Serpent Ring!' hisses the creature. 'Its power will not save your life, Analander, but I am bound by its power to aid you. I will tell you this: pay respect to Naggamanteh the torture master should you meet him. But that is all I am bound to tell.' Now return to **303** and choose your next course of action.

290

A wide smile spreads across the little creature's lips. 'How did you know?' it demands. 'How did you know I have been looking for one of these?' Your lucky choice has been a success. But something is not quite right. The creature's voice is changing as it speaks to you to that of a middle-aged woman. 'Such a friend should not be teased,' she says. And with these words, her form changes to that of a tall woman dressed in purple robes. 'I am Dintainta,' she starts, 'Dintainta of the Steppes. Though some call me The Sham. I know of your mission and I can help you. It is a credit to your wit and your courage that you have survived this far. But much greater dangers lie ahead. At the Fortress of Mampang, beware the Sleepless Ram, for even your skill will be no match for its powers. You will overcome it by uncorking this vial in its presence.' She hands you a small glass vial. 'Guard this vial with your life and let no one release the gas within. I will also tell you this: a short distance ahead you will confront the Earth Serpent. His powers are considerable, but these powers exist only when he is in contact with the earth. Perhaps this information will help you defeat the beast. Finally, I give you this in exchange for your gift.' She hands you her walking stick. 'My Serpent Staff is enchanted and will give you powers against the Serpents. And now I must leave you, as I must journey home before sundown.' She turns herself back into the ugly little creature you first encountered and sets off on her way. This has been a lucky encounter (you may add 2 LUCK points). Her Serpent Staff will weaken any of the Serpents you come across. You may deduct 2 SKILL points from any Serpents you fight while carrying this stick. You notice also that it has been carved from an Oak Sapling, so may be used in your spells. The creature has by now disappeared in the distance and you turn to make your way onwards. Turn to **114**.

291

Treat the Flying Fish as a single creature:

FLYING FISH   SKILL 8   STAMINA 8

If you defeat them, turn to **75**.

292

The Marsh Goblins pause in the clearing just long enough to catch their breath and then hurry off, still looking behind them as they go. You must now decide whether to wait again, perhaps to find out if anything was following the Goblins (turn to **105**), or to leave the area (turn to **270**).

293

You start rowing across the wide lake. The water is thick and heavy, making your journey quite a tiring exercise (deduct 1 SKILL point until you reach the shore). The ferryman is silent, watching you as you struggle with the oars. You speak to him, but he does not reply. His expression is vacant; his eyes glazed. Again you try to speak to him, but there is still no response. Something is not quite right here. You rest your oars and reach forward to shake him. As your hand touches his shoulder, to your horror the ferryman's body shrivels and slumps down, falling over the seat like a limp sack! At the same time, a hissing noise catches your attention. A jet of gas has escaped from the soulless body and hovers in the air in front of you. As it swirls around, it gradually forms the shape of a winged snake. When the shape has formed, it begins to circle in the air above you, dropping lower and lower towards you. A pungent, choking smell hits your nostrils and you must react quickly. Will you draw your weapon to fight the creature (turn to **261**) or cast a spell?

ZAP	KIN	SIX	DUM	HUF
363	419	482	464	350

Or will you instead ignore the creature and see what has happened to the ferryman (turn to **21**)?

294

The Black Elves watch as you leave the camp. To your great relief they allow you to go without trouble. Turn to **269**.

295

You continue cautiously through the reeds and grasses until a loud rustling noise to your right makes you stop. The rustling turns into a loud hissing and a large snake-like head rises into the air above the vegetation. It swivels to the left and right as if looking for something. But when its eyes fall on you, steam hisses from between its fangs and it flaps its wings. It rises into the air and circles over you, preparing to strike. What will you do – draw your weapon (turn to **103**) or cast a spell (turn to **53**)?

296

The medicinal potions are not what you expected. The small vial that the sorceress has given you contains a liquid which will not work with spells. However, it is capable of curing any diseases you might pick up on your journey. Add 2 LUCK points for this find. Now turn to **92** to leave the Elf's home.

297

Word for word, you repeat the spirit's chant. Silence settles over the area – an unnatural silence. Will this strange luck deity show itself to you? Clouds move quickly, yet silently across the sky. Suddenly a loud crack breaks the stillness, followed by a bolt of lightning which sparks from the heavens to the ground where the Seven Spirits have been. They have disappeared! You call out for them in a threatening voice, but your threat cannot conceal the fear you are trying your best to mask. The spirit voice returns, but this time a mocking laugh fills the air. The voice circles round and round you, laughing loudly until it gradually fades. As it does so, a soft woman's voice calls to you, a voice which sounds familiar: 'They have tricked you! The evil spirits have been sent by the Archmage and you have fallen into their trap! In innocence you have thrice damned my name with their chant. I cannot help you in what is to follow.' As your goddess's voice fades, the laughter reappears. The spirit's face appears in front of you. Its mouth opens in a mocking grin and, as it does so, the face swells in size, growing until it is soon the size of your body. Still the face grins and the laughter rings in your ears. Ringing, laughing, mocking, laughing . . . you hold your hands over your ears to shut out the noise. The face is now twice your size and, as you look into its cavernous mouth, you are suddenly caught! A long, red, snake-like tongue darts from its throat. It wraps itself around you swiftly and you are jerked inside the mouth. Into the blackness you plunge.

You do not emerge from the spirit's throat. Whether your fate is death or a life in limbo will never be known. But one thing is certain. You will never again return to this plane of life.

298
You agree to her terms and bow down to her image on the statue. She will allow you to leave the temple without further injury, but the price is high. Never again during your quest for the Crown of Kings will you be able to call on help from Libra. You are on your own in Kakhabad! You may now leave the area. Turn to **309**.

299
You leave the caravan. Oolooh follows you to the door with a sour face. Outside, the old Elf and a small crowd are gathered. 'Bah!' shouts Oolooh. 'My time has been wasted! For this niggardly creature offers nothing for our treasures. See the Horntoad off, Cesstar!' Turn to **288**.

300
As you stand to leave, your foot dislodges a chunk of rock, which scuttles off down the slope. Half-way down, it stops unnaturally and *reverses direction*! It rolls towards you and you watch in amazement as it bumps painfully into your ankle (deduct 1 STAMINA point). You reach down to rub it and, as you do so, a rumbling shakes the ground and knocks you off balance. The peak of the rock explodes into the air, erupting like a volcano and spraying stones everywhere. Will you run to try to avoid the falling rocks (turn to **30**) or cast a spell?

DOZ	MAG	WOK	FOG	HUF
453	378	477	447	428

301
You climb down into the pit to talk to the Snake Charmer. He seems a little *too* friendly and you are not certain whether to trust him or not. The snakes are all watching you but have not moved. He asks about the artefacts you have collected on your travels and would like you to show him some. Will you open up your pack to show him what you have inside (turn to **87**) or will you refuse and instead ask him questions about himself (turn to **108**)?

302

The moonless night makes your journey hard going as it is difficult to see anything around you. But the night passes and at dawn you are once again able to see your way clearly. Deduct 2 STAMINA points for continuing through the night and another 3 STAMINA points if you did not eat at all yesterday. Which direction do you now wish to continue in? Will you head north-east (turn to **15**) or north-west (turn to **217**)?

303

Without warning, the bubbling starts again, this time on the port side of the boat. Breaking through the surface of the water, a shape rises into the air. A snake-like coil rises from the lake on watery wings and hovers, dripping, in the air. This creature is made from water itself and it glares down at you, ready to strike. Will you cast a spell?

WOK	FOF	RAZ	MUD	HOT
436	493	414	473	385

Or will you fight it another way (turn to **172**)?

304

Half an hour later there are still no signs of intelligent life around the lake shore. In fact, if you have arrived at this reference, it is likely that you will wait for a very long time for the means to cross Lake Ilklala. It *is* possible to cross the lake, but only if you can summon the ferryman. If you do not know how to summon him, this is as far as you will get in this adventure.

305

The Stranglebush is squeezing you tighter and tighter. Your struggles are wasted and it soon becomes difficult to breathe. You cannot move your arms, so you cannot cast a spell. If you are to survive this encounter, you have but one hope left: a prayer to Libra. If you have not yet called on your goddess in this adventure, turn to **56**. Otherwise your journey has come to an end.

306

Getting back to the trail, you follow it until you reach a fork. Will you take the left fork (turn to **244**) or the right fork (turn to **214**)?

307

As you rise from the crevice, the small green snake once more wraps itself around your leg. The answer dawns on you! You must kill the little creature! Turn to **263**.

308

The rumblings get louder as you find a suitable crevice which will afford at least *some* shelter for you. You wait for the rain to start falling and prepare yourself using your leather tunic as a cover. But rain does not fall. Instead, the wind returns and this time in a swirling gale! Frantically, you grab hold of your belongings in case they are whipped away from you by the furious dust storm. You shield your eyes and face from its abrasive gusts, but the force is tremendous. Roll one die to see what fate befalls you:

Roll
1–2	Turn to **44**
3–4	Turn to **141**
5–6	Turn to **219**

309

From here you may continue either due north (turn to **149**) or north-eastwards (turn to **15**). Which direction will you choose?

310

Which spell will you choose?

NAP	MAG	FIX	DIM	SUS
470	452	433	487	424

If you know none of these you will have to face the creature with a weapon. Will you use a normal weapon (turn to **32**) or a silver weapon (turn to **84**)?

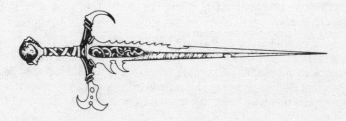

311

Your suspicions are aroused. You follow him carefully towards the caravan. Then your opportunity comes. You dart between two carriages and out of the camp. The Black Elves scream and several archers ready their bows and fire at you as you flee. Roll one die. This is the number of arrows that they unleash as you make your escape. For each arrow, you must *Test your Luck*. If you are *Lucky*, the arrow misses. If you are *Unlucky*, the arrow will strike and wound you. The first three arrows (or less than three if you rolled a low number) will inflict 2 STAMINA points of damage. If you rolled higher than three, any subsequent arrows will only do 1 STAMINA point of damage as you will then be further away. Once you are out of range, you may choose your direction. Turn to **269**.

312

The man runs into a corner of the pit and puts his pipe to his lips. You rush towards him to finish him off, but as you advance, a strange feeling comes over you. Turn to **248**.

313

As you draw your weapon, they grab bows, notching arrows pointed at you. You stare at one another and you must now choose your next move. Will you drop your weapon and quickly cast a spell (turn to **175**) or throw yourself into their midst and attack (turn to **70**)?

314

The Nighthawks circle and prepare for another attack. Suddenly the formation breaks and their cries take on a different tone. *Something* has disturbed them and they seem to be in a state of confusion. But you can see nothing.

A moment later, a shape forms in the air in their midst. The Nighthawks shriek as a GOLDCREST EAGLE materializes and lashes out at them with its deadly beak. Your spirits rise at your good fortune. Goldcrest Eagles are raised and trained in Analand as birds of war. But what is this great Eagle doing so far from its home?

The Eagle snaps its razor-sharp beak through one of the Nighthawks and plucks at another with its talons. The two remaining birds turn to the west and dart away to safety. With the threat dispersed, the Eagle drops down to land by you. Around its neck is a small tube containing a message, sealed with the Royal Seal of the King of Analand, which you unroll and read:

We trust these tidings reach you in fair health, but must warn you of impending peril. Your mission is discovered!

The Mampang's eyes have spied our plan and word is on its way to the dark fortress. Too late we discovered our unwelcome eavesdroppers and news of your quest is being carried towards High Xamen by Seven Serpents, the Archmage's most trusted servants. By now they will have reached the Baklands and here they will divide to complete their journey separately.

If you are still able, seek them out, for they must stop to rest and eat. Destroy the creatures before they reach their goal, else the Archmage will prepare a deadly welcome for you.

Find Shadrack the Hermit for advice, for naught moves through the Baklands without his knowledge.

Our hearts are with you.

You look back at the great bird which has brought this welcome warning, but it is no longer with you. Having delivered its message, it will no doubt be winging its way back to Analand, flying safely under a shroud of invisibility.

Studying the message again, you stuff it into your tunic. The instructions are wise. If your mission is to succeed, you must undoubtedly find and destroy the Archmage's messengers before word of your arrival reaches Mampang. Turn to **48**.

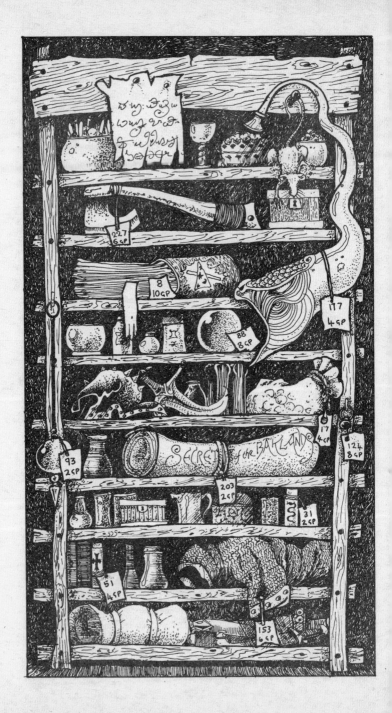

The old Elf leads you into the centre of the camp where a large caravan stands. Its door is guarded by two armed Elves. 'Tell Oolooh we have a customer,' he orders one of the guards, who climbs into the caravan to report your arrival. A skinny black face appears at the door. 'And what sort of a bargain-hunter can we have happened across here in the middle of Baddu-Bak?' asks the face. 'Aha! A human! Well, come inside, come inside. Let's see what bargains we can strike with one another, eh? Come on, come on!' He waves you inside and you follow. Your eyes light up as you enter the caravan. It is a veritable treasure trove of valuables, magic items and equipment. Oolooh looks up at you over half-moon eyeglasses. He is flicking through a catalogue of some kind. 'And what is your art, stranger? Weaponry? Sorcery? Are you a craftsman? Or how about some fine treasures for gifts at the end of your journey? We have it all. And at fair prices, too!' You pause to look over his shelves while he chatters away at you. 'How about piece number 227, a fine Hewing Axe? Very useful if you are heading northwards. And only 6 Gold Pieces. Or piece number 93, a Brass Pendulum? Always hangs down, and no lodestone can deflect it. 2 Gold Pieces to you. Or a fine Pearl Ring – piece number 124 – a gift fit for a king? But that'll cost you 8 Pieces. Or a bag of Vittles . . . let's see . . . yes, piece number 17. Ideal provisions for long journeys. Only 4 Gold Pieces for the whole bag.'

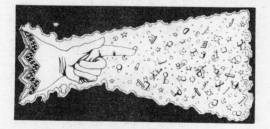

If you have any Gold, you may buy from him anything you wish on his shelves. If you would prefer to barter, you may select anything (except your weapon) you have with you and offer it in exchange. Roll two dice for each of the items you are offering to test your bartering skill. If the number you roll is greater than your SKILL score, the Black Elf is not interested in that piece. If the roll is equal to your SKILL score, he will assign a value of 3 Gold Pieces to your offering. You may exchange it for anything priced at up to 3 Gold Pieces, or offer it together with something else if you want something costing more than 3 Gold Pieces. If the roll is lower than your SKILL, then the Elf will value it at a higher price. He will accept its value as 3 Gold Pieces *plus* the difference (in Gold Pieces) between your SKILL and the die roll. For example, if your SKILL is 7 and you roll a 5, this item is worth 3 Gold Pieces *plus* the difference (2), that is, 5 Gold Pieces in exchange for anything he has to offer.

If you have nothing to offer, or do not wish to barter here, turn to 299. If you do buy anything, you may find out what it is by turning to the reference with the same piece number as your purchase.

316

The noises get louder and louder until a group of three Marsh Goblins breaks through into your clearing. You stand and face each other. They are snub-nosed, ugly creatures with webbed fingers and they are evidently most surprised to see you. Do you wish to draw your sword (turn to 194), talk to them (turn to 208) or cast a spell?

GOB	NIF	POP	RAP	NIP
459	331	484	396	347

317

She scoffs: 'Do you think I would help one who planned to hold a weapon against me? I will tell you nothing. Begone! And quickly, before you once more feel Fenestra's power!' She looks towards you and her wide eyes begin to glow like coals. You decide it best not to risk seeing what she may have in mind for you and return to the door. Outside, you rejoin the path and continue your journey. Turn to 92.

318

You continue along the trail in a north-westerly direction. Turn to **47**.

319

You pull your Borrinskin boots out of your pack and start to put them on. The Serpent slithers around in the branches above, watching you. Before you can put on the boots, it drops down from the tree and wraps itself around you! You manage to hurl it off, but you must now fight the creature:

FIRE SERPENT   SKILL 13   STAMINA 12

If you win the battle, turn to **306**.

320

You pray desperately to Libra and dodge the falling stones as you wait for her help. Another stone grazes your leg – lose 1 STAMINA point. You begin to hear a soft musical voice from within your head, calling out your name. The goddess is answering you! You listen: '. . . You are one of my most loyal subjects and I dearly want to help you in your mission. But even a god may not help if a prayer comes from the temple of another god. Indeed this is an *insult* to the gods. I know your prayer was innocent and for this I forgive you. But I cannot help you with this danger . . . '

You curse. Of course! It is blasphemy to call on one god from the temple of another. But while you curse, another stone lands on your head and knocks you reeling – lose 3 STAMINA points. How will you get out of here? Will you pray instead to the goddess of the temple (turn to **206**) or will you open the trapdoor (turn to **156**)?

321

At the kitchen tent you are introduced as a wealthy traveller who wishes to buy food. Their menu is simple. For 6 Gold Pieces, you will get a bowl of Whortle soup, followed by Gloister and bread, with a cup of herb tea. If you can afford this, pay your money and turn to **163**. If you can't afford it, or if you don't wish to buy, turn to **192**.

322

You leave the rock and head across the steppes. Will you head in a north-westerly direction (turn to **149**) or a north-easterly direction (turn to **73**)?

323

You command them to reveal their true selves to you. They stand in silence. You ask them to name their gods. Again, silence. But a transformation is taking place. Under their cowls, something is happening, but their faces are hidden so you cannot see what. You order them to show themselves! Slowly, each phantom lifts its hands to its hood. Together they flip back their cowls and the sight revealed makes you freeze in terror! Each spirit now has the head of a hissing serpent, darting and flashing in your direction! In blind panic you burst from the circle and run towards the forest, not daring to look backwards. The shock will cost you 1 SKILL point. When you are a safe distance from them, you slow down. Ahead of you is the next stage of your quest: the Forest of the Snatta. Turn to **133**.

324

Before you leave, Fenestra offers to help you by giving you a gift. She can offer:

A medicinal potion	Turn to **296**
A lucky charm	Turn to **195**
A calling-whistle	Turn to **221**

You may choose one of these. Turn to the reference indicated to find that item's effect. Turn also to **221** if you collected a whistle earlier from Fenestra.

325

You drop to the ground in agony. The leader of the Horsemen strides over and kicks you with his hoof. Seeing that you are in no position to retaliate, he bends down and goes through your possessions, helping himself to all of them. The Horsemen leave you for dead. But you are not quite dead yet. After a short rest you may stagger on, but you have now lost all of your artefacts and your Provisions. Turn to **273**.

326

Mercilessly, you step over to deliver the final blow. Your opponent slumps to the ground. He will frighten unwary adventurers no more. You turn him over with your foot. As you touch him, something happens which makes you freeze. Turn to **143**.

327

You draw your weapon and shout at the ungrateful creature, telling it to give you back the gift. 'But I *never* give back my gifts,' it laughs. 'A gift is not a gift if it has to be given back!' This makes you angry and you rush at the creature. It makes a swift motion with one finger, pointing at your feet. Your boots seem to take on minds of their own and you trip over, falling head first on to the ground. Your forehead strikes a bare rock and you lose consciousness. Lose 3 STAMINA points. You wake up a short while later and the creature is nowhere in sight. Turn to **114**.

328

A crack of thunder above you confirms your fears. *The storm is following you!* You stop to look for any likely shelter, but there is none to be found. The storm is about to break and you have no alternative but to wrap yourself up and plod on through it. Turn to **247**.

329

The path is quite wide and looks well used. But there are no signs of who, or what, uses it. For most of the morning, you follow it through the woods until you reach an area where two paths converge. Further on from that, the path becomes much narrower. You are following a little-used trail – yet this is definitely the way towards Lake Ilklala. You squeeze between two bushes which have overgrown the path and find yourself tangled up in them. This is most annoying and you try to pull yourself free. A chill comes over you. You are getting tangled further! The bush itself seems to be wrapping around you! In a short time you will not be able to move – what will you do? Draw your weapon (turn to **167**) or cast a spell?

NIP	GOB	ROK	FIX	HOT
466	346	368	448	387

If you have any Essence of Bark with you, you may turn to **212**. If you have a Hewing Axe with you, turn to **196**.

330

The soft voice of a woman reaches your ears. You look around but can see no one. 'Be not afraid,' it whispers. 'You cannot see me but I am with you. I come to warn and advise you. For the scroll you have found is a valuable aid, but one which a warrior such as yourself could not hope to understand. Scribed on this parchment is a chant which will render powerless the Serpent of Time. Use it and you need not fear the creature. That is all I can tell you, except for this: if you encounter the Serpent, do not try to fight it with your weapon or magic. Instead hold up the scroll and recite the chant to the best of your ability.' The voice disappears and you unroll the parchment. You will find an illustration of this chant on the page facing reference **410**. If you encounter the Serpent of Time and can make any sense of this chant, it will suggest to you a reference number. Turn to this reference number instead of fighting the Serpent. Now return to **270** and continue.

331

Deduct 1 STAMINA point. You cast your spell and create a horrendous stench which swells up and engulfs the area. The Marsh Goblins' noses twitch and you wait to see their reactions. But to your dismay, these foul creatures *like* the stink you have created! But do *you* have any nose plugs? If not, the smell will make you ill for a few moments (lose 3 STAMINA points) and force you to leave the area – turn to **168**. If you have nose plugs, you will be safe from harm and you may choose either to fight the Goblins (turn to **194**) or run from them (turn to **168**).

332

Deduct 4 STAMINA points. You cast the spell, but nothing happens, as this spell will only work on non-intelligent creatures. Return to **49** and choose again.

333

Deduct 1 STAMINA point. Do you have a Staff of Oak Sapling with you? If not, you cannot use this spell and the Bear attacks, causing 2 STAMINA points of damage – turn to **139**. If you have such a Staff, you may hold it up and cast your spell. The Bear will stop immediately in its tracks, held immobile. You may take your time and continue your journey. Turn to **20**.

334

Deduct 1 STAMINA point. Do you have a Sun Jewel? If not, deduct 3 STAMINA points as the Beetle attacks while you are trying to make the spell work, and turn to **286**. If you have a Sun Jewel, your spell will cause it to glow brightly straight into the Beetle's eyes. You increase the brightness until the creature backs off. As you correctly deduced, it is an underground creature which cannot tolerate bright lights. The Beetle retreats into its hole and disappears underground. Turn to **24**.

335

Deduct 2 STAMINA points. Your spell will protect you from any magic in the area. But it is not magic which is causing the destruction of the temple. Again you must jump to avoid being hit by falling rocks, and again you land painfully. Lose another 2 STAMINA points and turn to **135**.

336

Deduct 2 STAMINA points. You cast your spell and are protected for a short time from any damage you would normally sustain through falling. You may now either draw your weapon and climb the tree (turn to 42 but if you do so, you will not suffer the penalties described) or you may search for another means of attack (turn to 197).

337

Deduct 4 STAMINA points. Your spell creates a magical barrier in front of you. The Nighthawks cannot break through this wall, but they are easily able to fly around it. Your plan will not stop them. Turn to 258.

338

To your credit you have dispatched four of the Archmage's servants, a feat beyond the abilities of most mortals. However, the other three Serpents are now travelling ahead of you to Mampang to warn of your arrival. You will need your wits about you in the final stage of your mission. Turn to 498.

339

Deduct 1 STAMINA point. Do you have a Green-Haired Wig with you? If not, this spell will not work. If you do have a Green-Haired Wig, you place it on your head and cast the spell, talking to the little snake. The snake does not reply. You had better draw your weapon and fight it (turn to 52).

340

Deduct 2 STAMINA points. Secretly, you cast your spell at the Champion and wait for it to take effect. Sure enough, his ferocity subsides and his expression changes from one of anger to a calmer, almost peaceful, look. But the fight must go on. Turn to 280 and resolve your battle with him, but you may reduce his SKILL by 3 points because of your spell.

341

Deduct 2 STAMINA points. You cast your spell and this will protect you from any magical traps that the Elves may have in store for you. Now will you follow the old man (turn to 151) or plan an escape (turn to 311)?

342

Your achievement has been great. Conquering five of the Archmage's Serpents is a feat worthy of a true champion of Analand. However, the remaining Serpents are already flying on ahead of you to warn their master of your whereabouts, and your mission. But your own survival across the Baklands has built up your confidence and your stamina. Restore your STAMINA to its *Initial* level and turn to 498.

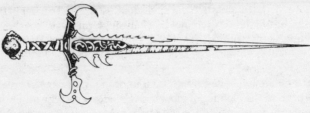

343

Do you have any Goblin's teeth with you? If not, your spell will not work and, whilst you try to cast it, two gashes appear on your arm as the Snattacats strike – deduct 3 STAMINA points, draw your weapon and turn to 99. If you have any Goblin's teeth, you toss two of them on the ground and cast your spell on them (deduct 2 STAMINA points). Two Goblins appear before you and you command them to attack the Snattacats. But since their opponents are invisible, and Goblins are pretty stupid creatures, the Snattacats are easily able to kill them. Now you must either draw your weapon and fight them yourself (turn to 99) or run away (turn to 246).

344

Deduct 1 STAMINA point. Do you have a Gold-Backed Mirror with you? If not, you cannot use this spell and the creatures will attack as you try it in vain – lose 2 STAMINA points and turn to 188. If you have a Gold-Backed Mirror, you may hold it up and start to cast your spell. *Test your Luck*. If you are *Lucky*, turn to 381; if you are *Unlucky* turn to 365.

345

Deduct 2 STAMINA points. You cast the spell and you are now safe from any magic which may be in the air. Unfortunately, there *is* no magic around you. Meanwhile, the Beetle attacks and catches you unawares. Deduct another 2 STAMINA points for your bruises and draw your weapon. Turn to 286.

346

Do you have any Goblin's teeth with you? If not, your spell will not work – turn to **305**. If you have any Goblin's teeth, you may cast your spell on them to create Goblins who will aid you. Deduct 1 STAMINA point for each tooth you use (each one will create a single Goblin). Any Goblins you create will help to disentangle you from the Stranglebush. To determine whether or not you manage to free yourself, throw one die and add to your roll the number of Goblins aiding you. If the total of the two is 6 or more, you free yourself (turn to **106**). If the total is less than 6, then the plant causes you 2 STAMINA points of damage and you may try again, losing two STAMINA points each time you are unsuccessful. Once you have started trying to free yourself, you may not create any more Goblins, so make sure you have enough to disentangle you!

347

Deduct 1 STAMINA point. Do you have any Yellow Powder with you? If not, this spell will not work; as you try to run off the Goblins grab you – draw your weapon and turn to **194**. If you have any Yellow Powder, you may sniff this and cast your spell to give you the power of swiftness – turn to **168** to run away from the area.

348

Deduct 1 STAMINA point. Do you have any medicinal potions or Blimberry juice with you? If not, turn to **236**. If you have either of these, your spell will take its healing effect. You may restore your STAMINA to its *Initial* level and you had now better get out of this pit. Turn to **211**.

349

Deduct 4 STAMINA points. You cast your spell and send a ball of flame flying towards the Fox. As your fireball hits, the flame bursts – but the Fox is unharmed! Draw your weapon and turn to **256**.

350

Deduct 1 STAMINA point. Do you have a Galehorn with you? If not, you cannot use this spell – turn to **395**. If you have a Galehorn, you may cast your spell and blow on the horn. A tremendous blast of wind comes from the horn aimed straight at the Air Serpent you face. It tries desperately to avoid the gust, but is caught and its shape disappears as its wispy body is dispersed. You have defeated the creature! Turn to **213**.

351

Deduct 1 STAMINA point. Do you have a Galehorn with you? If not, your spell will not work and while you try in vain to cast it, the Serpent strikes, causing 3 STAMINA points of damage – draw your weapon and turn to **54**. If you have a Galehorn, you may cast your spell and blow the horn. A tremendous gust of air blasts from the horn which catches the Serpent's wings and lifts it into the air. Turn to **127**.

352

Deduct 1 STAMINA point. Do you have any stone dust with you? If not, you cannot use this spell. If you have some, you can throw it on the Demon and cast your spell. However, since the Demon is already made of stone, your spell is ineffectual. Whether or not you had any stone dust, deduct 2 STAMINA points as a blow from the Rock Demon catches you unawares. Then draw your weapon and turn to **268**.

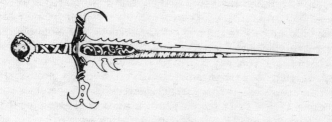

353
Deduct 1 STAMINA point. Do you have a Bamboo Pipe? If not, the spell will not work – turn to **248**. If you have a pipe, you start to play and cast your spell. A smile spreads over the man's face. 'Sssoo, my ssissterss,' he laughs. 'Our visssitor isss alssoo a musssician.' But his reaction is not what you'd expect from the spell; it is having no effect on him. For he is also a master of the magic pipe and his tune is reaching out to you. Turn to **248**.

354
Deduct 1 STAMINA point. Do you have an Orb of Crystal with you? If not, you cannot use this spell – return to **171** and choose again. If you have a Crystal Orb, turn to **492**.

355
Deduct 4 STAMINA points. You cast your spell and a lightning blast shoots from your finger at the snake. The little creature is vaporized. You may now leave the area. Turn to **309**.

356

Deduct 1 STAMINA point. Do you have a Jewel of Gold with you? If not, this spell will not work and you will be attacked as you fumble with it – lose 2 STAMINA points and turn to **188**. If you have a Jewel of Gold, you may wear it and cast your spell. The creatures stop advancing and their expressions turn from anger to interest. They lower their clubs and grunt at you. You cannot understand their language (if indeed it *is* a language) but you exchange a few words in sign language until they turn to go. You may now continue. Add only 1 STAMINA point for the night's rest as your sleep was disturbed, and deduct 3 STAMINA points if you ate nothing yesterday. Now you can collect your things and leave. Will you head north-west (turn to **83**), north-north-west (turn to **283**) or straight ahead northwards (turn to **60**)?

357

You have defeated the Seven Serpents! You are indeed a worthy champion of Analand. Your success now means that you may continue your journey to the fortress at Mampang unannounced: the Archmage will not have been warned of your arrival or your mission. In view of this, you may start your next adventure in *The Crown of Kings* at reference **237** instead of reference **1**. You may also increase your SKILL to 2 points above its *Initial* level (this now becomes your permanent *Initial* SKILL score). Your STAMINA can be restored to its *Initial* level. You may increase your *Initial* LUCK score by 1 point and restore your LUCK to this new level. Now turn to **498**.

358

Do you have any Goblin's teeth with you? If not, your spell will not work and while you try to cast it, two gashes appear on your arms as the Snattacats strike – deduct 3 STAMINA points, draw your weapon and turn to **74**. If you have Goblin's teeth, you toss two on the ground and cast your spell on them (deduct 2 STAMINA points). In a flash, two Goblins have appeared and you command them to attack the Snattacats. However, since they cannot *see* their opponents, their attacks will not help and the Snattacats are easily able to kill them. You must draw your weapon and turn to **74**.

359

Deduct 1 STAMINA point. Do you have a Galehorn with you? If not, you cannot cast your spell – return to **97** and choose again. If you have a Galehorn, you cast your spell and blow through the horn. A whistling sound gets louder and louder until a blast of wind explodes from the horn towards the strange enigma before you. It strains to hold its position but the force of your blast sends it flying into the distance. You may now choose your way onwards. Turn to **322**.

360

Deduct 1 STAMINA point. Do you have any beeswax with you? If not, your spell will not work and while you fumble with it, the Flying Fish attack, causing 2 STAMINA points of damage – turn to **291**. If you have some beeswax, you may rub it on your weapon and cast the spell. Now turn to **291** and fight the creatures, but during this fight, your weapon will inflict double damage (4 STAMINA points instead of the normal 2).

361

Deduct 1 STAMINA point. Do you have a Green-Haired Wig with you? If not, your spell will not work and the Bear attacks – deduct 2 STAMINA points and turn to **139**. If you have a Green-Haired Wig, you may place it on your head, cast your spell and try to talk to the Bear. But there is only one message you can get from the creature: it is hungry and wants food! Return quickly to **244** and choose again.

362

Deduct 1 STAMINA point. Do you have a Giant's tooth with you? If not, you cannot use this spell – return to **115**. If you can cast your spell over a Giant's tooth, the magic creates a burly Giant before you. You command the Giant to break apart the rock and free you. It struggles valiantly in spite of the burning heat underfoot. Within a few moments, it has managed to dislodge a rock and your leg comes free. Its job now done, the Giant disappears. Turn to **307**.

363

Deduct 4 STAMINA points. You cast your spell and a bolt of lightning shoots from your fingertip at the creature – and then right through it! This spell will not help you here. Turn to **395**.

364

Deduct 2 STAMINA points. You cast your spell and realize your wasted effort. You are already in darkness. Why should you want to cast this spell? The Serpent is amused at your blunder and it takes advantage of the situation, attacking swiftly. Lose 2 STAMINA points and draw your weapon. Turn to **45**.

365

As you cast the spell, one of the creatures throws its club at the Mirror, knocking it out of your hands on to the ground. It lands awkwardly and shatters. The Mirror is now of no use and you will have to leave it behind. Draw your weapon and turn to **188**.

366

Deduct 2 STAMINA points. You cast your spell and wait for its 'inner advice' to warn you of any impending danger. Sure enough, the old Elf is leading you into a trap. You may either go along with him and plan to nip off out of this place at a suitable time (turn to **311**). Or you may instead tell them that you would like to buy Provisions from them, hoping that a little Gold will override their suspicions (turn to **215**).

367

Deduct 2 STAMINA points. Your spell has no effect on the Serpent as it is designed to cause attackers to fumble with weapons and other objects. You will have to face it with your weapon. Turn to 54.

368

Deduct 1 STAMINA point. Do you have any stone dust with you? If not, you cannot use this spell – turn to 305. If you have some stone dust, you may sprinkle it over the STRANGLEBUSH and cast your spell. However, this spell will not work on plants and you will have to draw your weapon to try to cut yourself free. Turn to 167.

369

Deduct 1 STAMINA point. Do you have any stone dust with you? If not, you cannot use this spell. If you have some dust, you may cast your spell on it and throw it at something (anything you like). Whatever it is turns to stone, but this does not help your plight. Whether or not you could cast the spell, your preoccupation with it has distracted you and you do not notice a large rock fall. It lands on your back. Lose 3 STAMINA points and turn to 135.

370

Deduct 2 STAMINA points. You cast your spell on a nearby rock and it turns into a small pile of treasure. The Baddu-Beetle, though, is not impressed and ignores your illusion. It swings a great claw and knocks you reeling. Deduct 2 STAMINA points. You decide it best to fight on with your weapon. Turn to 286.

371

Deduct 1 STAMINA point. Do you have any sand with you? If not, your spell will not work – turn to 236. If you have some sand, you may throw it on to the hot rock and cast your spell. Your magic creates a pool of quicksand around the rock and it begins to sink into the earth once more, bubbling and boiling. As it disappears you have a chance to lift yourself out of the pit. Turn to 43.

372

Deduct 1 STAMINA point. Do you have any beeswax with you? If not, this spell will not work although you will *think* it has worked – turn to **268** to fight the Demon, but deduct 1 SKILL point as you will be slightly overconfident. If you have any beeswax, you must also turn to **268**, but the spell will sharpen your blade so that any successful hits will do 4 STAMINA points of damage instead of the normal 2.

373

Deduct 1 STAMINA point. Do you have a Staff of Oak Sapling with you? If not, your spell will not work and the fish will attack, causing 2 STAMINA points of damage (turn to **291**). If you have an Oak Staff, your spell will affect a small number of the Flying Fish, holding them suspended in the air. But the majority of the fish will still attack. Turn to **291** but you may deduct 1 SKILL point from the fish.

374

Deduct 1 STAMINA point. Do you have any glue with you? If not, return to **272** and choose another course of action. If you have some glue, you may cast your spell and throw the vial of glue on to any object you like. This object then becomes stuck firmly in position. Cross the vial of glue off your Equipment List and return to **272** to choose again.

375

Deduct 1 STAMINA point. Whether or not you have a Sun Jewel, this spell is no help to you in your predicament. Return to **115** and choose again.

376

Deduct 1 STAMINA point. Do you have a vial of glue with you? If not, you cannot use this spell and you will be attacked by the Snattacats as you try to get it to work – deduct 3 STAMINA points and turn to **99**. If you have a vial of glue, you may throw it at a Snattacat and cast your spell. But since the creatures are invisible, it will be a matter of luck whether it hits one or not. *Test your Luck*. If you are *Lucky*, you manage to catch one of the advancing Snattacats and only three will attack; if you are *Unlucky*, you miss them. Now turn to **99** to fight them.

377

Deduct 4 STAMINA points. You cast your spell and a burning fireball appears in your palm. The Moon Serpent pulls back and watches you carefully, waiting for your move. Quickly, you fling the fireball at it! It darts to one side, trying to avoid being hit, but the fireball strikes it. The Serpent squeals in agony. Turn to **62**.

378

Deduct 2 STAMINA points. You cast your spell and wait for it to take effect, to protect you from any magical traps. Although something supernatural is indeed happening, your spell is not powerful enough to protect you from the forces at work here. Return to **300** and choose again.

379

Deduct 1 STAMINA point. Do you have a Staff of Oak Sapling with you? If not, you cannot use this spell – return to **49** and choose again. If you have an Oak Staff, you may cast the spell and freeze the ferryman where he stands, refusing to release him unless he agrees to ferry you across without charging you. Eventually he agrees. Turn to **110**.

380

Deduct 2 STAMINA points. You cast your spell and wait for it to take effect. Nothing happens! This spell may only be used in a closed room, not in the open air. While you are waiting, one of the Nighthawks darts in and gashes your cheek with its beak. Deduct another STAMINA point. You had better draw your weapon before they attack. Turn to **258**.

381

As you cast the spell, one of the creatures throws its club at the Mirror, knocking it from your hands on to the ground. You hold your breath but, as luck would have it, the glass does not break and you will be able to pick it up again at the earliest opportunity. Turn to **188**.

382

Deduct 1 STAMINA point. Do you have a Gold-Backed Mirror with you? If not, your spell will not work and the Rock Demon hits you for 3 STAMINA points of damage as you wait for something to happen. If you have a Gold-Backed Mirror, you hold it to face the Demon and cast the spell. In front of you stands an exact duplicate of the Demon and you command it to attack. Turn to **268** to conduct the battle. Remember that your duplicate Demon has the same SKILL and STAMINA as the original. While the two Demons are battling it out, you may attempt to free yourself each Attack Round. If your creation loses, you will have to finish off the battle yourself.

383

Deduct 4 STAMINA points. You cast your spell and create an invisible field around yourself which the Snattacats cannot penetrate. Eventually they give up trying to reach you and leave the area. Turn to **160**.

384

The spell takes effect. 'One moment,' says the old Elf. 'It is not often that we have visitors here. What say we extend our hospitality to our guest?' The crowd nod in agreement. 'Come, stranger, come and try a bowl of Whortle soup. One of our specialities!' You follow him to a kitchen tent. Inside, the cook brings you the soup. Turn to **163**.

385

Deduct 4 STAMINA points. You cast your spell and create a series of small fireballs which you hurl at the creature. Your aim is true, but your missiles extinguish themselves as soon as they come into contact with the Water Serpent. Turn to **172** and choose another method of dealing with it.

386

Although you have defeated one of the Serpents, the other six have escaped you and are now flying hard towards the Mampang Fortress to warn their master of your impending arrival. To your credit, you have survived the journey so far, but your failure to defeat the Serpents means you will need all your courage and wits about you in the final stage of your mission. Deduct 2 SKILL points, 1 STAMINA point and 2 LUCK points in view of this, and turn to **498**.

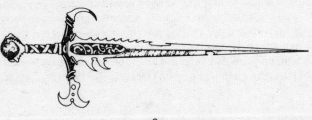

387

Deduct 4 STAMINA points. You cast your spell and create a fireball in the palm of your hand. But as you try to decide on a place to attack, you realize that this method of attack is too risky to yourself. Since the STRANGLEBUSH has wrapped itself all around you, there is nowhere you can effectively burn it without possibly burning yourself! You had better try instead to pull out your weapon. Turn to **167**.

388

Deduct 1 STAMINA point. Do you have a Bracelet of Bone with you? If not, you cannot get the spell to work – turn to **248**. If you have a Bracelet of Bone, you place it on your wrist and cast your spell. You concentrate on the illusion that the Snake Charmer's pets are escaping, slithering away out of the pit. The man drops his pipe and goes running after his snakes. This will delay him just long enough for you to look round the pit. But you will have to be careful; the real snakes are still there! Turn to **260**.

389

Deduct 1 STAMINA point. Do you have any sand with you? If not, you cannot use this spell – return to 97 and choose again. If you have some sand you may throw it on the ground underneath whatever it is in front of you and cast your spell. But nothing happens. The strange enigma in front of you is not actually touching the ground so is unaffected by the quicksand which you have created beneath it. Do you wish to investigate it more carefully (turn to 157) or ignore it and continue (turn to 322)?

390

Deduct 4 STAMINA points. Your spell takes effect and you are surrounded by a protective aura. However, it can do nothing to free your leg. Return to 115 and choose again.

391

Deduct 2 STAMINA points. You cast your spell and it affects one of the Horsemen, who shakes his head and looks dumbly at the others. Now is your chance to leap to the attack. Turn to 70. But the Horseman under your spell (you choose which one) will not join in the fight and you may kill him easily once you have finished with the other two.

392

Deduct 1 STAMINA point. Do you have a Bracelet of Bone? If not, you cannot use this spell. But even if you have a Bracelet of Bone, your spell is not powerful enough to affect the Moon Serpent. Whether or not you can cast this spell, it does not work and the Serpent strikes. Lose 2 STAMINA points, draw your weapon and turn to 45.

393

Your long trek across the Baklands is almost over. Having left the Vischlami Swamps, you now stand at the Zanzunu foothills from where you will climb through Xamen to the Fortress at Mampang. But will your arrival be anticipated? How many of the Seven Serpents have you either killed or left trapped, unable to warn the Archduke of your mission?

No Serpents?	Turn to 496
One Serpent?	Turn to 386
Two Serpents?	Turn to 479
Three Serpents?	Turn to 444
Four Serpents?	Turn to 338
Five Serpents?	Turn to 342
Six Serpents?	Turn to 435
Seven Serpents?	Turn to 357

394

Deduct 1 STAMINA point. Do you have a Jewel of Gold with you? If not, your spell will not work and you must follow the old Elf – turn to 151. If you have a Jewel of Gold, turn to 384.

395

The swirling shape closes in around you, trying to choke you! Deduct 2 STAMINA points and decide quickly what your next action will be. Will you draw your weapon and try to fight the creature (turn to 261), will you see if there is anything you can do to help the ferryman (turn to 21), or would you like to try another spell?

DUM	KIN	SIX	HUF	ZAP
464	419	482	350	363

396

Deduct 1 STAMINA point. Do you have a Green-Haired Wig with you? If not, you cannot use this spell and must choose either to run away from the Goblins (turn to 168) or to draw your weapon and fight (turn to 194). If you have a Green-Haired Wig, turn to 410.

397

Deduct 4 STAMINA points. You cast your spell and create around you an invisible shield. The snake is not able to penetrate your shield and eventually it slithers off. You may now leave the area. Turn to **309**.

398

Deduct 1 STAMINA point. Do you have a Pearl Ring with you? If not, this spell will not work; you will not become invisible, but you will *believe* that you are – turn to **74** to face the Snattacats but deduct 2 points from your SKILL during this battle. If you have a Pearl Ring you may cast this spell and, under your cloak of invisibility, you may leave the area. Turn to **271**.

399

Deduct 1 STAMINA point. Do you have any small pebbles? If not, you cannot cast this spell. If you have any such pebbles, you may cast your spell over them and throw them at the door. They hit the door and explode with a loud bang, but the door itself is sturdy and remains unaffected. Return to **171** and choose again.

400

Deduct 1 STAMINA point. You cast your spell and a horrendous stench fills the air. The Fox sniffs the air. The smell reaches its nostrils and it howls in horror of the stink. With its tail between its legs, it turns and races off into the distance. But the smell will also affect you. Do you have any nose plugs? If not, the foul stench will make you ill and cause 3 STAMINA points of damage. If you do, you will not be affected. You may now leave. Turn to **95**.

401

Deduct 2 STAMINA points. As the spell takes effect, you get the strong feeling that the hieroglyphics conceal a trap – you would be well advised to avoid them. If you wish to open the trapdoor, turn to **180**. If you wish to look around a bit more, turn to **101**. If you ignore the warning and read the hieroglyphics anyway, turn to **189**.

402

Deduct 1 STAMINA point. Whether or not you have the Holy Water necessary to perform this spell, it will do you no good, as its effect is to bring the dead back to life. So far, no one has died! But seeing you try to cast the spell angers the Klattaman Champion and he strikes you with his wooden club. The blow causes 3 STAMINA points of damage. You had better draw your weapon and turn to **280**.

403

Deduct 1 STAMINA point. Your spell creates a disgusting stench which surrounds your boat. But, alas, this smell has no effect on the Flying Fish. Do you have any nose plugs with you? If not, the spell will affect *you* as the smell hits your nostrils and you must deduct 3 STAMINA points. Now draw your weapon and turn to **291**.

404

Deduct 2 STAMINA points. This spell will not work outdoors. Return to **49** and make another choice.

405

Deduct 1 STAMINA point. Do you have a Bamboo Flute with you? If not, you cannot use this spell. If you do have such a flute, you cast your spell and play the instrument. But to your dismay, the Serpent is unaffected by your spell (whether it works or not) and instead darts at you to attack. Lose 2 STAMINA points and draw your weapon (turn to 45).

406

Deduct 1 STAMINA point. Whether or not you have the Staff of Oak Sapling you need for casting this spell, it will be of no use to you. As the heat increases you must deduct 2 STAMINA points and turn to 236.

407

Deduct 4 STAMINA points. You cast your spell and send a flaming fireball hurtling towards the little snake. With a flash, the snake disappears, leaving a charred skeleton behind. You may now leave the area. Turn to 309.

408

Deduct 2 STAMINA points. You cast your spell and a mental bell starts ringing in your head to warn you of this character. His music is enchanted! Your best bet is either to cooperate with him or to leave as quickly as possible. If you wish to cooperate, you may offer to show him what you have in your backpack (turn to 87). If you wish to leave, you may turn away from him and quickly leave the pit (turn to 318). Otherwise, you can simply listen to the tune he is playing (turn to 248).

409

Deduct 4 STAMINA points. You cast your spell and point at the door, sending a bolt of lightning shooting towards the lock. With a loud crack, the door shudders and swings on its hinges. Turn to 265.

410

You place the Wig on your head, cast your spell and start to talk to the Goblins. Their incomprehensible jabberings begin to sound more meaningful and soon you are talking to them. You manage to establish that they are running from a great Serpent. They believe it has godly powers, but you explain it is likely to be one of the Archmage's messengers. They had been trying to drive the creature from the area with the help of a sacred scroll given to them by the sorceress from the Forest of the Snatta. But they could not read the scroll and couldn't decide what to do with it. You ask for a look at the scroll and one of them pulls it out. The language on the scroll is strange and the message is written in the form of a short magic spell or chant.

You study the chant and can begin to make some sense of it. Look at the message illustrated. It may suggest to you a reference number. When you come across the Serpent of Time, you will most likely die unless you can pick up a clue, in the form of this reference number, from this chant. If you face the Serpent of Time, turn to this reference (no option will be given) and, if you are correct, you will be able to defeat the creature.

You thank the Goblins for their information and promise to do what you can to destroy the Serpent. Turn to **295**.

411

Deduct 4 STAMINA points. You cast your spell and create a fireball in the palm of your hand, hurling it upwards at the Serpent. The creature hisses as your missile bounces off, without damaging it at all. In fact you find you have to leap aside to avoid it! Will you now draw your weapon and climb the tree (turn to **42**), choose another means of attack (turn to **197**) or leave the creature alone and move on (turn to **306**)?

412

Deduct 5 STAMINA points. There is no such spell as this. Return to **189** and choose again.

413

Deduct 2 STAMINA points. You cast your spell and you are now protected from magic. Unfortunately, the Moon Serpent attacks non-magically and it strikes you. Deduct another 2 STAMINA points and turn to **45**.

414

Deduct 1 STAMINA point. Do you have any beeswax with you? If not, you cannot use this spell and, sensing your confusion, the Serpent strikes – deduct 3 STAMINA points and turn to **172**. If you have some beeswax, you may wipe it on your weapon and cast the spell. Now turn to **172**. If you choose to fight the creature, your weapon will do extra damage. As the Serpent is made of water, this will be 3 STAMINA points instead of the normal 2.

415

Deduct 2 STAMINA points. You cast your spell and create six identical images of yourself. The Bear stops and examines each one, trying to decide which to attack. It makes its choice, and to your horror, it has chosen the correct image! Draw your weapon and turn to **139**.

416

Deduct 1 STAMINA point. Do you have a Green-Haired Wig with you? If not, this spell will not work and the Fox will attack (lose 2 STAMINA points, draw your weapon and turn to **256**). If you have a Green-Haired Wig, you can place it on your head and use your spell to communicate with the creature. However, it is not interested in talking to you and can think only of food. It sees you as its next meal! Draw your weapon and turn to **256**.

417

Deduct 2 STAMINA points. You cast your spell and create a magical barrier in front of you which nothing may penetrate. But your suspicions were misguided. Nothing happens which may have made your wall useful. Return to **272** and choose your next course of action.

418

Deduct 5 STAMINA points. There is no such spell as this. Turn to **236**.

419

Deduct 1 STAMINA point. Do you have a Gold-Backed Mirror with you? If not, you cannot use this spell. But even if you have such a Mirror, you are horrified to find that the swirling Air Serpent you are facing casts no reflection! Turn to **395**.

420

Deduct 1 STAMINA point. Do you have a Black Facemask with you? If not, your spell will not work – the Klattaman strikes you with his club (deduct 2 STAMINA points) as a challenge and you must turn to **280** to fight him. If you have a Black Facemask, you hold it before your face as you cast the spell. The tall Klattaman starts to look worried. Moments later he is positively terrified! He turns to run from you and, amid hisses and jeers from the others, disappears into one of the huts. The onlookers look suspiciously at you and you decide it best to take your leave. Turn to **173**.

421

Deduct 1 STAMINA point. Do you have a Green-Haired Wig with you? If not, you cannot cast this spell – return to **97** and choose again. If you have a Green-Haired Wig, you place it on your head and wait for the spell to take effect. You try talking to the oddity. Nothing happens. Return to **97** and choose again.

422

Deduct 2 STAMINA points. You cast your spell at one of the Horsemen. He looks at his bow and drops it down on the ground. The other two stare at their companion, who now gazes vacantly into space. You seize your opportunity to attack:

First HORSEMAN	SKILL 1	STAMINA 7
Second HORSEMAN	SKILL 7	STAMINA 6
Third HORSEMAN	SKILL 7	STAMINA 8

Fight the Horsemen one at a time, in reverse order. Once you have killed the first two, you may allow the last one to surrender if you wish. If you do so, turn to **35**. If you want to finish them all off, turn to **154**.

423

Deduct 1 STAMINA point. Do you have an Orb of Crystal with you? If not, your spell will not work and the Snattacats will attack you, causing 3 STAMINA points of damage – turn to **74**. If you have an Orb of Crystal, you may hold it up and cast your spell on to it. Within the ball, you can discern shapes which you can eventually make out as yourself and a number of Snattacats approaching you! By reading the ball, you can know in advance where the creatures are coming from, and with this information, you are able to avoid them and continue onwards safely. Turn to **271**.

424

Deduct 2 STAMINA points. You wait apprehensively as the spell takes effect. The Deathwraith in front of you is not so much a trap as an illusion. But you feel strong indications of impending danger involving a reptile of some sort. You may challenge the creature in front of you with a normal weapon. Turn to **32**.

425

Deduct 1 STAMINA point. Do you have a scullcap with you? If not, you cannot use this spell. If you have a skullcap, you may place it on your head, cast your spell and wait for any indication the spell may give about this place. You receive no such psychic messages. Return to **171** and choose again.

426

Deduct 4 STAMINA points. You cast the spell in the nick of time, creating a solid invisible barrier between you and the attacking fish. The Flying Fish collide into your wall and drop back into the sea, unable to attack you. Turn to **75**.

427

Deduct 1 STAMINA point. You cannot use this spell as you do not have the Yellow Powder it requires. Meanwhile, the Snake Charmer has been playing. Turn to **248**.

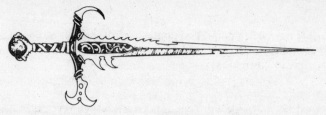

428

Deduct 1 STAMINA point. Do you have a Galehorn with you? If not, you cannot use this spell and a shower of stones lands around you causing 2 STAMINA points of damage – turn to **30**. If you have the Galehorn, you can use the spell to create a tremendous wind which you hope will blow the falling rocks away from you. However, the wind will blow in one direction only and is not a great deal of use here. Turn to **30**.

429

Deduct 4 STAMINA points. You cast your spell and an invisible barrier forms around you. Falling stones bounce off your protective shield. Large rocks cause it to shudder, but it holds fast. Some time later, the spell wears off. Turn to **9**.

430

Deduct 4 STAMINA points. The birds prepare to attack as you cast your spell. But when it affects them, they stop in the air as if waiting for some command. You order them to fly off southwards. They wheel in the sky and start to fly back towards the Cityport. But soon they stop as the spell wears off and they return to attack again. Turn to **314**.

431

Deduct 1 STAMINA point. Do you have any stone dust with you? If not, you try desperately to petrify the Snattacats but your spell will not work – deduct 3 STAMINA points as one attacks you, draw your weapon and turn to **99**. If you have some stone dust, you may try to immobilize three of the Snattacats which are attacking you. *Test your Luck*. If you are *Lucky*, your attempt is successful: the three invisible creatures are turned to stone statues, leaving only the fourth for you to fight. If you are *Unlucky*, you only manage to catch one of the creatures, leaving three for you to face. Draw your weapon and turn to **99**.

432

Deduct 1 STAMINA point. You cannot use this spell as you do not have the Brass Pendulum you need to cast it. You follow the old Elf towards the caravan. Turn to **151**.

433

Deduct 1 STAMINA point. You cannot use this spell as you do not have the Staff of Oak Sapling it requires. While you try to make it work, the Deathwraith slashes at you with its long fingers. It catches your cheek, inflicting 2 STAMINA points of damage. You quickly draw your weapon. Turn to **32**.

434

Deduct 1 STAMINA point. You cast your spell and a foul, putrid stink swells up around you and rises up towards the creature. Do you have a pair of nose plugs with you? If not, the smell will overcome you and you must lose 3 STAMINA points through nausea. If you have nose plugs, you may put them in quickly and avoid any illness. But the smell does not affect the Serpent sitting up in the tree. Return to **123** and choose again.

435

You have crossed the Baklands and defeated six of the Archmage's servants – a feat truly worthy of a champion of Analand. But the last Serpent, undefeated, is now winging its way towards its master and will arrive at Mampang ahead of you to warn him of your mission. Nevertheless, your success so far has filled you with great confidence. You may restore your SKILL and STAMINA scores to their *Initial* levels. If the only remaining undefeated Serpent is the Sun Serpent, turn to **458**. Otherwise, turn to **498**.

436

Deduct 1 STAMINA point. Do you have a coin with you? If not, this spell will not work. If you have a coin, you may place it on your wrist and cast the spell. The coin will transform itself into an invisible shield. Turn to **172**. If you fight the Serpent, your shield will allow you to deduct 2 points from the creature's Attack Strength.

437

Deduct 4 STAMINA points. You cast your spell and the Bear stops in its tracks at your command. You order it to turn and go, and it does so. Turn to **20**.

438

Deduct 1 STAMINA point. Do you have an Orb of Crystal with you? If not you must return to **115** and choose again. If you have a Crystal Orb, your spell will have its effect. The Orb begins to swirl with colours and, as they clear, you can see a rocky crag. It is the area you are in! But cracks in the ground are healing up and the shower of stones is subsiding. The area is returning to normal. But what does this mean? This information certainly cannot help you at the moment. Return to **115** and choose again.

439

Deduct 1 STAMINA point. Do you have a Bracelet of Bone with you? If not, you cannot use this spell and while you are trying to make it work the creatures attack – lose 2 STAMINA points and turn to **188**. If you have a Bracelet of Bone, you slip it over your wrist and cast your spell. Before their eyes, you turn into a great Horned Demon, belching smoke and flames from your nostrils. You guessed correctly. These primitive creatures are very superstitious and they have taken your transformation as a sign that their gods are displeased with them. You command them to hand over their possessions and then be gone. Terrified, they do as you ask. Turn to **251**.

440

Deduct 2 STAMINA points. The Beetle stops as you cast your spell and grow in size before it. You may attack it now at double your normal SKILL. Turn to **286** and resolve your combat.

441

Deduct 1 STAMINA point. Do you have any medicinal potions or Blimberry juice with you? If not, the spell will not work. If you have either of these, you may either use them on yourself, or offer to administer them to the ferryman. If you use them on yourself, you may restore your STAMINA to its *Initial* level, then return to **49** to choose your next course of action. If you offer them to the ferryman, he will agree to ferry you across the lake for nothing – turn to **110**.

442

Using your spell, you penetrate the old Elf's mind. Clearly he is leading you into a trap if you follow him. But you can tell that they are traders and will be more than interested in Gold Pieces. Will you tell him that you are more interested in buying Provisions (turn to **215**) or that you too are a trader and would like to see what they have to offer (turn to **315**)?

443

Deduct 1 STAMINA point. Do you have a Brass Pendulum with you? If not, your spell will not work and the Serpent will attack for 3 STAMINA points of damage; you must then draw your weapon and turn to **54**. If you have a Brass Pendulum, you begin to swing it, your spell focusing the Serpent's attention on the metal bob. But, alas, this spell is not powerful enough to overcome the will power of the great Serpent. It strikes the pendulum from your hand (this is now lost) and attacks. You must draw your weapon. Turn to **54**.

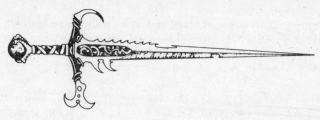

444

With three Serpents defeated, you can justifiably feel satisfied with your valiant attempt to prevent them warning their master of your arrival. But your effort has not been good enough and the Archduke will be making plans to welcome you in his own special way. In view of this, you must deduct 1 SKILL point. Now turn to **498**.

445

Deduct 2 STAMINA points. You cast your spell and wait for it to take effect. While you are waiting another arrow shoots towards you. Roll one die. A 1–3 indicates a hit, for 2 STAMINA points of damage. The Horsemen load up their bows again. Your spell is useless in this situation! You had better attack them quickly. Turn to **70**.

446

Deduct 2 STAMINA points. As you cast the spell, an inner voice tells you to beware of this enigma in front of you, for it is dangerous and has nothing to offer you. You are safe if you keep your distance, but you must not get too close. Turn to **157**.

447

Deduct 2 STAMINA points. You cast your spell. But nothing happens! You cannot use this spell outdoors and, while you are trying to make it work, you are showered with stones. Lose 1 STAMINA point and turn to **30**.

448

Deduct 1 STAMINA point. Do you have with you a Staff of Oak Sapling? If not, your spell will not work and you must turn to **305**. If you have such a Staff, you may cast the spell on the STRANGLEBUSH to hold it fixed in place while you work yourself free. Turn to **106**.

449

Deduct 1 STAMINA point. Do you have a Potion of Fire Water with you? If not, the spell does nothing and the fish attack (for 2 STAMINA points of damage) while you are trying to work it – turn to **291**. If you have a Potion of Fire Water, you may drink this and cast your spell. Immediately you feel a surge of strength fill your body, with power swelling your muscles. However, there are so many fish that your extra strength is not going to be a great deal of use here. Turn to **291** and resolve this combat.

450

Deduct 1 STAMINA point. You cannot use this spell as you do not have the Crystal Orb it requires. As you try to make it work, his tune reaches you. Turn to **248**.

451

Deduct 1 STAMINA point. Do you have a vial of glue? If not, this spell will not work and you must lose an extra 3 STAMINA points as the Snattacats attack – turn to **74**. If you have a vial of glue, you may throw it on the ground and cast your spell on it. But since the Snattacats are invisible, it will be a matter of luck whether any of them step on the glue and are held by it or not. Turn to **74** and follow the instructions. But you may, if you wish, *Test your Luck* here. If you are *Lucky*, the glue will catch one of the attacking Snattacats and hold it, so you will fight one less than the number you will be told to roll. If you are *Unlucky*, the Snattacats will all pass by your trap.

452

Deduct 2 STAMINA points. You cast your spell and wait to see whether anything happens. The shimmering haze reappears and engulfs the creature once more. As it rises, the Deathwraith is being transformed and another shape now stands before you. A stout, balding man appears in its place, who looks at you nervously and smiles. The Deathwraith has been an illusion! You may now fight the creature:

BALDING MAN   SKILL 6   STAMINA 9

If you win, turn to **143**. If you would prefer to spare the man's life, turn to **72** instead.

453

Deduct 2 STAMINA points. Your spell would be effective against an attacking creature, but it is useless against a shower of rocks! Turn to **30**.

454

Deduct 4 STAMINA points. Your spell creates an invisible shield around you that the Snattacats cannot break through. You can continue unharmed through the area, leaving the creatures behind. The spell eventually wears off at a clearing where you may rest briefly. Turn to **20**.

455

Deduct 4 STAMINA points. Your spell sends a flash of lightning from your fingertip towards the Demon. But since it is made of rock, the blast has no effect. Return to **185** and make another choice.

456

Deduct 1 STAMINA point. Do you have a Black Facemask with you? If not, this spell will not work and the creatures will attack as you try to use it – deduct 2 STAMINA points and turn to **188**. If you have a Black Facemask, you may hold it up before your face and cast your spell. The spell will create a fear in their minds which will be to your advantage in the battle which you will have to fight. Turn to **188** but you may deduct 2 points from the creatures' Attack Strength rolls while they are in this fearful state.

457

Deduct 4 STAMINA points. Quietly you cast your spell and command the Klattaman to hold his ground. But your plan has not worked! This spell only works on non-intelligent creatures! Draw your weapon and prepare for battle. Turn to **280**.

458

Whether or not you realize it, the Sun Serpent has been captured and will not be able to escape to warn the Archduke of your mission. You may ignore the bonuses granted on the last reference and instead turn to **357**.

459

Do you have any Goblin's teeth with you? If not, you may not cast this spell – draw your weapon and turn to **194**. If you have any Goblin's teeth, you may drop as many as you wish on the ground and cast your spell (deduct 1 STAMINA point per tooth used). The teeth grow into armed Goblins which you may then command to attack. Your own Goblins have a SKILL of 5 and a STAMINA of 5. Turn to **194** and resolve the combat. Resolve the battle in the normal way on a one-against-one basis as far as possible, but any spare Marsh Goblins will attack you rather than your Goblin creations.

460

Deduct 4 STAMINA points. You cast your spell and point a finger towards the creature, sending a bolt of lightning shooting towards it. However, since it is entwined in the branches of the tree, you cannot get a direct aim at it and your blast is absorbed by a branch. Return to **123** and choose another course of action.

461

Deduct 1 STAMINA point. Do you have a Green-Haired Wig with you? If not, this spell will not work – draw your weapon and turn to **52**. If you have a Green-Haired Wig, you may place it on your head and cast your spell. You call out to the little snake and it stops, looking up at you. 'Great beast with two legs,' it hisses. 'You wake me. Stay away. I bite.' You explain that you do not wish to harm it. 'Leave me,' it orders. Will you leave it, fight it or cast another spell? Return to **23** and choose again.

462

Deduct 4 STAMINA points. You prepare your spell and cast it cautiously, as you are exposing yourself to what could be a dangerous situation. You aim your blast quite close to yourself, hoping that the lightning bolt will break up the ground. Your plan succeeds! Your leg comes free. Turn to **307**.

463

Deduct 1 STAMINA point. You cannot cast this spell as you do not have the Staff of Oak Sapling it requires. While you are waiting for something to happen, two of the Nighthawks dart down at you and their sharp beaks gash your skin. Deduct 2 STAMINA points and turn to **258**.

464

Deduct 2 STAMINA points. This spell *would* work, but it is not appropriate here as the Air Serpent you face is carrying no weapon. Turn to **395**.

465
Deduct 1 STAMINA point. Do you have any medicinal potions or Blimberry juice with you? If not, the spell will not work – return to **272** and choose again. If you have either of these, you may cast the spell and take one measure of the potion. Within moments you will begin to feel revitalized as the healing spell takes effect. Restore your STAMINA to its *Initial* level. Then return to **272** and choose again.

466
Deduct 1 STAMINA point. Do you have any Yellow Powder with you? If not, your spell will not work. If you have any Yellow Powder, you must sniff some and you may then cast your spell. However, the STRANGLEBUSH is holding you firm and your actions, although speeded up to several times their normal rate, cannot disentangle you. Turn to **305**.

467
Deduct 1 STAMINA point. Do you have a Crystal Orb with you? If not, you cannot use this spell and must draw your weapon – but the Snattacats will attack immediately (deduct 3 STAMINA points and turn to **99**). If you have a Crystal Orb, you may use your spell to read the future. Looking into the Orb you can see yourself with the Snattacats and can thus see where they are advancing from. Using this information, you may avoid the creatures easily. Turn to **41**.

468
Deduct 2 STAMINA points. You cast your spell. But nothing happens! This spell may only be cast indoors and is useless here. Meanwhile, the Fox springs at you and attacks: deduct 2 STAMINA points. Now you must draw your weapon and face it. Turn to **256**.

469
Deduct 2 STAMINA points. You cast your spell and the door opens. Turn to **265**.

470

Deduct 1 STAMINA point. You cannot use this spell as you do not have the Brass Pendulum it requires. As you try in vain to make it work, the Deathwraith slashes at you with its bony fingers, catching you across the cheek and inflicting 2 STAMINA points' worth of damage. You had better draw your weapon and turn to **32**.

471

Deduct 1 STAMINA point. Do you have a Jewel-Studded Medallion with you? If not, you cannot use this spell and the Serpent attacks for 3 STAMINA points of damage – turn to **54** and face it with your weapon. If you have a Jewel-Studded Medallion, you may wear it and cast the spell as the Serpent strikes. You begin to rise into the air and, by grabbing the Serpent, you may lift it up with you. Turn to **127**.

472

Deduct 1 STAMINA point. Do you have a cloth skullcap with you? If not, your spell will not work – follow the Elf and turn to **151**. If you have a skullcap, turn to **442**.

473

Deduct 1 STAMINA point. Do you have any grains of sand with you? If not, this spell will not work and the Serpent strikes as you fumble with it – lose 3 STAMINA points and turn to **172**. If you have any grains of sand, this spell will still not do you any good. The Serpent, being made of water, will not be trapped by quicksand, even if you can find some way of getting them in contact with one another. You have wasted your grains of sand and must now turn to **172**.

474

Deduct 1 STAMINA point. Do you have a Galehorn with you? If not, you cannot use this spell – draw your weapon and climb the tree (turn to 42). If you have a Galehorn, you may cast your spell and use the Galehorn to produce forceful blasts of wind. You may face the Fire Serpent with your weapon (turn to 42) and if you do so you will be immune from any special damage caused by its power of fire *and* you may add 2 SKILL points as you fight it (but only during this battle). Otherwise you may leave the creature alone (turn to 306).

475

Deduct 1 STAMINA point. Do you have a Giant's tooth with you? If not, you cannot cast this spell and as you fumble with it one of the creatures lands a blow on you – lose 2 STAMINA points and turn to 188. If you have a Giant's tooth, you toss it on the ground. You are about to cast your spell when one of the creatures grabs it from the dirt and puts it in its pocket! It seems to regard your tooth as a valuable object. Draw your weapon and turn to 188.

476

Deduct 2 STAMINA points. You cast your spell and wait for something to happen. Nothing does. Your spell is designed to open doors! Meanwhile, one of the Horsemen releases another arrow at you. Roll one die. A roll of 1–3 indicates a hit, for 2 STAMINA points of damage. Your only chance now is to charge at them while they reload their bows. Turn to 70.

477

Deduct 1 STAMINA point. Do you have a Gold Piece with you? If not, you cannot use this spell and while you are trying to cast it, you are hit by falling rocks for 2 STAMINA points of damage and must turn to 30. If you have a Gold Piece, you can cast your spell on it to form a magical shield which will protect you from the rock shower. Turn to 30. But using your shield, you will not lose any STAMINA points at that reference.

478

Deduct 2 STAMINA points. Your spell creates a small pile of treasure, but the Rock Demon does not even notice this distraction. Instead it swings its arm and catches you in the chest. Take 2 STAMINA points of damage and return to 185 to choose again.

479

You have survived the perilous journey across the Baklands, but you have only conquered two of the Archmage's servants. The other five Serpents are presently heading towards Mampang to warn him of your arrival. In view of this, you must deduct 1 SKILL and 1 LUCK point, for the next stage of your journey will be the most perilous of all. Turn now to 498.

480

Deduct 1 STAMINA point. Do you have a Jewel of Gold with you? If not, you cannot cast this spell – return to 49 and choose again. If you have a Jewel of Gold, you may wear it and cast the spell. As the spell takes effect, the ferryman's face softens. 'Ach, forget the money,' he says. 'I've nothing to spend it on here, anyway. Hold on there, I'll get the boat. I'll row yer across just for the company.' Turn to 110.

481

Deduct 1 STAMINA point. Do you have a Staff of Oak Sapling with you? If not, you cannot use this spell – a falling rock glances off your arm (lose 2 STAMINA points) and you must turn to 135. If you have a Staff of Oak Sapling, you may use it to cast your spell. As the spell takes effect, the rocks and stones begin to hold their positions, held fast by your magic. Turn to 9.

482

Deduct 2 STAMINA points. You cast the spell and six duplicates of yourself appear. You hope that this will confuse the Air Serpent you face, but your illusion is wasted. Within the narrow confines of the boat, all six duplicates must huddle together and it is a simple matter for the Serpent to swirl across the face of each. The *real* you is given away by your coughing. Turn to 395.

483

Deduct 1 STAMINA point. Do you have any sand with you? If not, you cannot cast this spell. But even if you do, the spell will do you no good, as the Nighthawks are not likely to get themselves trapped in a pool of quicksand. While you are concentrating, two of the birds dart down from the sky and their sharp beaks gash your skin (deduct 2 STAMINA points). Turn to 258.

484

Deduct 1 STAMINA point. Do you have any small pebbles with you? If not, you may not cast this spell and must instead draw your weapon and face the Goblins (turn to 194). If you have any small pebbles, you may cast your spell on these to turn them into lethal exploding missiles. Since the Goblins are so close, you cannot miss with your aim. You can kill them all and search their bodies (turn to 277).

485

Deduct 2 STAMINA points. You cast your spell and the Bear continues its advance, swiping at you with a paw and gashing your arm for 2 STAMINA points of damage. This spell will make a creature clumsy if it is carrying something but will not affect a Bear attacking unarmed. Draw your weapon and turn to 139.

486

Deduct 4 STAMINA points. Your spell creates an invisible field around you which nothing may penetrate. But this force-field will not keep out the heat of the hot rock by your feet. Turn to 236.

487

Deduct 2 STAMINA points. You cast your spell and the Deathwraith stops and shakes its head. It looks at you dumbly and then looks into the sky. Now is your chance to attack it. Draw your weapon and attack. While in its confused state, it will fight with:

DEATHWRAITH   SKILL 5   STAMINA 9

Each Attack Round you must throw one die. A roll of 1–4 means it will stay confused for the next Attack Round. A roll of 5 means it will return to normal (SKILL 9 and STAMINA 9) in the next Attack Round. A roll of 6 means it will return to normal in the next Attack Round *and* it manages to get in a lucky slash with its bony fingers for an extra 2 STAMINA points of damage. You may either decide to spare its life (turn to 205 when you have reduced its STAMINA to three or less) or finish it off (turn to 326).

488

Deduct 4 STAMINA points. You cast your spell and point your finger at the creature to unleash a powerful lightning blast at it. A bolt shoots from your fingertip straight at the creature. It bellows as the blast hits its mark, but rather than defeating the Beetle, your attack has instead only enraged it! Its tough, armoured body has not been harmed – and now it is very angry. Turn to 286 and conduct the battle, but during the first Attack Round, add 4 points to the Beetle's Attack Strength roll since it is now attacking you fiercely.

489

Deduct 1 STAMINA point. Do you have any small pebbles with you? If not, you may pick up one from the ground and cast your spell on it. The pebble is now charged and will explode on impact if you throw it. You may throw it wherever you like. Then return to 272 to choose your next course of action.

490

Deduct 1 STAMINA point. Do you have a Green-Haired Wig with you? If not, you cannot use this spell – return to 97 and choose again. If you do have such a Wig, you can place it on your head and cast your spell. You try talking to the whirlwind-like enigma in front of you. But you receive no replies. Perhaps it cannot hear you. Turn to 157.

491

Deduct 2 STAMINA points. Although this spell would work on a lesser creature, its power is not great enough to overcome that of the Serpent. Return to 263 quickly and choose another spell.

492

You cast your spell and gaze into the Orb. You can see a dark, underground cavern with a table and chair at which a single human-like figure sits, gazing into a similar Crystal Orb! Something is swirling in this other Orb, but you cannot see what images are forming. What can this mean? Return to 171 and choose your next course of action.

493

Deduct 4 STAMINA points. You create a protective shield around yourself. The creature strikes – and passes right through your in-visible shield! You must quickly decide on another plan. Turn to 172.

494

Deduct 2 STAMINA points. Casting your spell on a nearby rock, it is transformed into a small pile of Gold Pieces. You wait for the Klattamen to realize. They notice the treasure, but are not at all interested! They are more excited about the prospect of a fight than about the Gold before them. Your spell has delayed the fight and the Klattaman Champion is angry. He swings his club and strikes you on the chest, winding you. This causes 2 STAMINA points of damage and you had now better draw your weapon. Turn to **280**.

495

Deduct 1 STAMINA point. You cannot cast this spell as you do not have the stone dust it requires. One of the Centaurs fires another arrow at you. Roll one die. A roll of 1–3 is a hit, for 2 STAMINA points of damage. After your poor attempt at sorcery, you will have to jump at them with your weapon. But hurry! They are already loading up their bows again. Turn to **70**.

496

All Seven Serpents are now winging their way to the Archduke's Fortress to warn him of your arrival. Preparations will be made to ensure that you do not reach your goal. Although you have survived the long journey across Kakhabad, many perils await you at Mampang. Because of this, you must deduct 2 SKILL, 2 STAMINA and 3 LUCK points. Now turn to **498**.

497

Deduct 1 STAMINA point. Do you have any glue with you? If not, the Fox snarls and springs, knocking you over for 2 STAMINA points' worth of damage – draw your weapon and turn to **256**. If you have a vial of glue, you throw it on the ground in front of the Fox. The creature comes over to sniff it and, as it does so, you cast your spell. As the creature's nose touches the glue, it binds tight, holding it firmly anchored to the ground by its snout. You may continue your journey. Turn to **95**.

You are relieved once more to step on to firm ground. You stand and survey the way onwards. Ahead of you lies the last stage of your quest: the climb up the Zanzunus to the Fortress at Mampang. You are now entering what must be Low Xamen. The going is uphill, but the dangers should be minimal as the rocky crags of Xamen are inhabited only by Birdmen. Soon the Fortress should be coming into view . . .

You continue onwards and upwards for several hours until the light begins to fade. As the sun sinks down the Zanzunu skyline, its dying rays light up a sight which you will remember for the rest of your days.

The sunset shadows make your first sighting of the Fortress a fearful one. Its tall spires and sharp angles give it a most intimidating look. One thing is certain: entering the Mampang Fortress will undoubtedly be the most perilous stage of your journey.

RULES FOR USING MAGIC

During your training you have been taught a number of spells and incantations which you use to aid you on your quest. The full list of spells follows these instructions.

Spells are identified by a three-letter word. Throughout the book you will be given the option of using spells to overcome problems and opponents. *The spells will be identified only by these three-letter words, so it is important that you memorize at least some of the codes.*

Thus, before you can start using your powers of sorcery, you will need to spend some time memorizing spells, as would a real wizard learning the magic arts. Obviously, you will not be able to memorize all forty-eight spells at once, but the more you use the book, the more familiar you will become with the most useful spells.

Try starting by memorizing between six and ten spells (the best ones to start with are given below) and relying on your swordsmanship to fight some of the creatures you encounter. It is possible, with a little luck, to complete your quest with these spells, but your task will become easier when you are capable of using more spells.

Some spells also require the use of an artefact, such as a piece of jewellery or a magic ring. If you try to use a spell without possessing the correct artefact, you will be wasting your STAMINA as the spell will not work.

Each time you use a spell – whether it is successful or not – it will draw on your reserves of energy and concentration. A cost, in STAMINA points, is given for each spell. Each time you use a spell, you must deduct this cost from your STAMINA score.

You may study the Book of Spells for as long as you want before embarking on an adventure, *but once you have set off, you may never again refer to it and must rely purely on your memory until your adventure is over.* Nor may you write the spells down for easy reference. In a real situation where you may be surprised by a creature, you would not have time to start flicking through your Spell Book trying to work out the best spell to cast!

The Six Most Useful Spells

Code	Effect	Stamina Cost
ZAP	Creates a lightning bolt which shoots from the fingertip	4
FOF	Creates a protective force-field	4
LAW	Enables creatures to be controlled	4
DUM	Makes creatures extremely clumsy	4
HOT	Creates a fireball which can be aimed at enemies	4
WAL	Creates a magic wall to defend against physical objects	4

ZAP and HOT are strong attacking spells, FOF and WAL are good general-purpose defensive spells, while LAW and DUM will be useful if you get into a tricky situation.

Note that these spells will often be more powerful than you need in a given situation – they are not cheap in terms of STAMINA points – but they are good all-rounders. As you get to know more spells from the Spell Book, you will be able to choose more economical spells which will be equally as effective against certain perils.

Read through the list again, then cover up the 'Effect' column with your hand. How many can you remember? When you can remember them by heart, you can begin your quest.

HINTS ON USING SPELLS

As you familiarize yourself with the spells in this Spell Book, your skill and abilities in the adventure will improve.

Learning the six basic spells will allow you to start playing with minimal delay. These spells will get you out of most difficulties, but they are expensive (in terms of STAMINA points) and you will often find it necessary to rely on your limited powers of swordsmanship, particularly with weaker creatures, in order to avoid running dangerously short of STAMINA.

Other spells are more economical but will be given less often as options, thus relying more on your memory and skill as a wizard. The most economical spells of all are those which require magical artefacts, which must be found on your adventure.

Remember that there are heavy penalties for guessing spells! If you choose a spell code which does not represent a spell, or if you choose a spell for which you do not have the required artefact, you will lose extra STAMINA points. In some cases, death will be your penalty!

Not all the spells are used in this adventure.

You will soon begin to make your own discoveries about the spells themselves. There is a certain logic to the way they are arranged, the options that are given and their codes. But these discoveries you must make for yourself. Experience will make you more skilful with magic. All this is part of the art of sorcery.

ZAP

An extremely powerful weapon, this spell creates a blast of lightning which shoots from the caster's hand, which must be pointed in the desired direction. It is effective against virtually all living creatures which have no magical defences. But it takes great strength and concentration to use.

Cost 4 STAMINA points

HOT

The caster may direct this spell with his hands in any direction desired. As it is cast, a burning fireball shoots from the hands towards its target. It will be effective against any creature, whether magical or not, unless that creature cannot be harmed by fire. The fireball so created causes severe burns on impact, but extinguishes soon after hitting its target.

Cost 4 STAMINA points

FOF

This powerful spell creates a magical and physical barrier in front of the caster which is capable of keeping out all physical intruders and most magical ones. Its creation takes excessive mental concentration but the resulting force-field is both extremely strong and is under the control of its creator's will, who can allow one-way penetration, or can position it as desired.

Cost 4 STAMINA points

WAL

The casting of this spell creates an invisible wall in front of the caster. This wall is impervious to all missiles, creatures, etc. It is a very useful defensive spell.

Cost 4 STAMINA points

LAW

Casting this spell at an attacking creature allows the caster to take control of the attacker's will. The attack will cease and the creature will immediately come under the control of the caster. However, this spell works only on non-intelligent creatures and lasts only for a short time.

Cost 4 STAMINA points

DUM

When cast at a creature holding an object of some sort (e.g. a weapon), this spell will make the creature clumsy and uncoordinated. It will drop the object, fumble to pick it up, drop it again – in short the creature is unlikely to do the caster any harm with any objects while under the influence of this spell.

Cost 4 STAMINA points

BIG

When this spell is cast on the caster's own body, it will inflate the body to three times normal size. This increases the power of the caster and is especially useful against large opponents, but must be used with caution in confined spaces!

Cost 2 STAMINA points

WOK

A coin of some sort is necessary for this spell. The caster places the coin on the wrist and casts the spell onto it. The coin becomes magically fixed on the wrist and acts as an invisible metal shield with an effective protection circle of just under three feet across. This will shield the user against all normal weapons. Afterwards, the coin is no longer usable as a coin.

Cost 1 STAMINA point

DOP

This spell may be used to open any locked door. Casting the spell works directly on the lock tumblers and the door may be opened freely. If the door is bolted from the inside, the bolts will be undone. The spell will not work on doors sealed by magic.

Cost 2 STAMINA points

RAZ

To perform this spell, beeswax is required. By rubbing the wax on any *edged* weapon (sword, axe, dagger, etc.) and casting this spell, the blade will become razor-sharp and do double its normal damage. Thus, if it normally inflicts 2 STAMINA points worth of damage, it will now inflict 4.

Cost 1 STAMINA point

SUS

This spell may be cast when the caster suspects a trap of some kind. Once cast it will indicate telepathically to the caster whether or not to beware of a trap and, if so, the best protective action. If caught in a trap, this spell may also be used to minimize its effects in certain cases.

Cost 2 STAMINA points

SIX

This spell is cast on to the caster's own body. Its effect is to create multiple images of the caster, all identical and all capable of casting spells and/or attacking, although each will perform identical actions as if reflected in a mirror. Most creatures faced with these replicas will be unable to tell which is the real one and will fight all six.

Cost 2 STAMINA points

JIG

When this spell is cast, the recipient gets the uncontrollable urge to dance. The caster can make any creature dance merry jigs by playing a small Bamboo Flute. If this flute has been found, the affected creature will dance for as long as it is played. This will normally give the caster time to escape – or he may continue playing and watch the show!

Cost 1 STAMINA point

GOB

This creation spell requires any number of teeth of Goblins. The spell may be cast on to these teeth to create one, two, or an army of Goblins.

These Goblins can then be commanded to fight an enemy or perform any duties they are instructed to carry out. They will disappear as soon as their duties have been performed.

Cost 1 STAMINA point per Goblin created

YOB

Casting this spell requires the tooth of a Giant. When this spell is cast upon the tooth correctly, a Giant, some twelve feet tall, will be created instantly. The caster has control over the Giant and may command him to fight an opponent, perform some feat of strength, etc. The Giant will disappear when his duty is done.

Cost 1 STAMINA point

GUM

Casting this spell, together with using the contents of a vial of glue, will cause the glue to become super-sticky, bonding in less than a second. Using the spell, the caster will be able to stick creatures to the floor or walls, although it is necessary to get the victim into contact with the glue from the vial. This can be done, for instance, by throwing it at the creature's feet, or by resting it on top of a slightly opened door, so that it falls when the door is opened.

Cost 1 STAMINA point

HOW

This spell is to be used in perilous situations when information about the safest way of escape is desired. When it has been cast, the caster will get an inclination towards one exit or, if a means of defence is present near by, will be directed towards it by a strange psychic force.

Cost 2 STAMINA points

DOC

Medicinal potions carried and used by the caster will, under this spell, have their effects increased so that they will heal any wounded human or creature who drinks them. The potions may be used on the caster – the spell must be cast as potion is being administered – but they will not bring a being who has actually died back to life.

Cost 1 STAMINA point

DOZ

This spell may be cast upon any creature, reducing its movements and reactions to about a sixth of its normal speed. Thus the creature appears to move as in a dream sequence, making it much easier to evade or defeat.

Cost 2 STAMINA points

DUD

By casting this spell, the caster can create an illusion of treasure in its many forms. Gold pieces, silver coins, gems and jewels can be created at will and these can be used to distract, pay off or bribe creatures. The illusionary riches will disappear as soon as the caster is out of sight.

Cost 2 STAMINA points

MAG

This spell protects its caster from most magical spells. It must be cast quickly, before the attacking spell takes effect. It works by neutralizing the attacking spell which disperses harmlessly. This spell is thus a very powerful protective weapon, but it does not work against every spell.

Cost 2 STAMINA points

POP

A potent little spell, but one which calls for great mental concentration, this spell must be cast on small pebbles. Once charged with magic, these pebbles can be thrown and will explode on impact. Apart from being dangerous to anything within shatter distance, the pebbles make a loud bang when they explode.

Cost 1 STAMINA point

FAL

This spell is useful if the caster is caught in a pit trap or falls from a considerable height. When cast, it makes the caster's body as light as a feather. The caster will float down through the air and land gently on the ground.

Cost 2 STAMINA points

DIM

A good defensive spell, this can be cast at any creature attacking the caster. Its effect is to muddle the mind of its victim, temporarily confusing the creature. However, it must be handled with caution, as a creature so deranged may act irrationally and unpredictably.

Cost 2 STAMINA points

FOG

This spell may only be cast in a closed room with no windows. Once cast, the room turns pitch black in the eyes of all but the caster – even though torches and candles may still be burning. It renders blind any creatures within the room. Its effects are only temporary.

Cost 2 STAMINA points

MUD

As this spell is cast, the caster must sprinkle grains of sand on to the floor as desired (e.g. in front of a creature). The spell takes effect on the sand and the floor, creating a pool of quicksand. Any creature stepping on this quicksand will slowly be drowned in it.

Cost 1 STAMINA point

NIF

As this spell is cast, the air surrounding the caster becomes filled with a nauseating stench. This smell is so horrible that it will cause any creature which catches a whiff of it to vomit violently. It will thus weaken any adversary with a sense of smell. This includes the caster unless he is wearing a pair of nose plugs. The effect will be more pronounced in creatures with large noses.

Cost 1 STAMINA point

TEL

To activate this spell, the caster must wear a cloth skullcap. With the aid of this cap, the spell will allow the user to read the mind of any intelligent creature encountered, learning about its strengths, weaknesses, the contents of nearby rooms, etc.

Cost 1 STAMINA point

GAK

In order to use this spell, the caster must be in possession of a Black Facemask, which must be worn while the spell is being cast. It can be cast directly on to an opponent and has the effect of creating a terrible fear within his mind. Brave creatures will be less affected than cowardly ones, so the effect varies from a cold sweat and loss of nerve to the creature's being reduced to a quivering jelly cowering in the corner of a room.

Cost 1 STAMINA point

SAP

The effect of this spell, which is only useful in combat, is to demoralize an opponent so that his will to win is lost. Any creature so demoralized will be easier to defeat – though victory is still not certain.

Cost 2 STAMINA points

GOD

This is a form of illusion spell which can only be performed if the caster is wearing a Jewel of Gold. When this spell is cast, any creatures or humans in the vicinity will take an immediate liking to the caster. This does *not* mean that they will not fight, if such is their duty, but they will be more likely to give information that they would not normally give. They may even help the caster in spite of their normally being hostile.

Cost 1 STAMINA point

KIN

This creation spell is useful in battles. It requires the use of a Gold-Backed Mirror, which must be pointed at a creature as the spell is cast. It creates an exact replica of any creature being fought and his double is under the control of the caster, who can instruct it to fight the original creature. Both will fight with the same strengths and weaknesses – only luck will separate their fates. If the original creature dies, its double will disappear. It will also disappear if it is defeated.

Cost 1 STAMINA point

PEP

A Potion of Fire Water must be taken by the caster for this spell to be used. It will enhance the effects of the Fire Water to give the caster double or treble his or her own normal strength. Although the effects are temporary, they will normally be enough to aid in battle or to perform some feat of super-strength.

Cost 1 STAMINA point

ROK

Stone dust is required for this spell. The dust must be thrown at a creature as the spell is being cast. Within seconds, the victim will start to petrify. As its movements become slower and eventually cease, it will start to turn grey. Some moments after the spell is cast, it will have solidified into a grey stone statue.

Cost 1 STAMINA point

NIP

The caster must cast this spell on his or her own body. Under the influence of this spell, the caster becomes exceedingly quick and may run, speak, think or fight at three times normal speed. However, this spell will only take effect if the caster sniffs Yellow Powder before using the spell.

Cost 1 STAMINA point

HUF

In order to use this spell, the caster must possess the Galehorn, a trumpet-like instrument which plays a discordant note. The spell is cast on to the horn and it is blown in a particular direction. As the spell takes effect, a tremendous wind rushes from the trumpet. This wind is capable of blowing over man-sized creatures, or it can be used to blow things off shelves, over ledges, etc.

Cost 1 STAMINA point

FIX

Applicable to both animate and inanimate objects, this spell has the effect of holding an opponent or object where it stands, unable to move even if in mid-air. In order to cast this spell, however, the caster must be holding a Staff of Oak Sapling. Anything held fast by this spell will remain frozen until the caster leaves the vicinity.

Cost 1 STAMINA point

NAP

Effective only against living creatures, this spell causes them to become drowsy and, within several seconds, to fall fast asleep. It is used in conjunction with a Brass Pendulum. The spell concentrates the creature's attention on the Pendulum, which the caster must swing slowly to and fro before the creature, in order to hypnotize it.

Cost 1 STAMINA point

ZEN

In order to cast this spell, the caster must wear a Jewel-Studded Medallion around the neck. Casting this spell will then allow the caster to float in the air at any height desired. A magician hovering thus will remain suspended for as long as desired and may float around at will.

Cost 1 STAMINA point

YAZ

This spell will not work unless the caster is wearing a fine Pearl Ring. Casting the spell while wearing this ring renders the caster's body invisible to any reasonably intelligent creature. It may be used to give considerable advantage in battle or to escape from a dangerous situation. Any creature with ears will be able to hear the caster as he moves around the room. Less intelligent creatures will only be partially convinced, as this is a form of illusion spell.

Cost 1 STAMINA point

SUN

This spell may only be cast upon the yellow Sun Jewel. Once cast, the Jewel begins to glow brightly. Its intensity is under the control of the caster, who can make it brilliant – in order to blind attacking creatures – or just light enough to act as a torch to see in dark rooms.

Cost 1 STAMINA point

KID

In order to use this spell, the caster must be wearing a Bracelet of Bone. Once the spell is cast, the caster must concentrate on a particular illusion (e.g. the floor is made of hot coals, the caster has turned into a Demon, etc.) and this illusion will appear real in the eyes of its intended victim. This may allow time for escape or lower a creature's defences. The spell will not work on non-intelligent creatures. If the caster acts in such a way as to destroy the illusion (e.g. turns into a mouse and then goes on to strike the creature with a sword), its effect will be lost immediately.

Cost 1 STAMINA point

RAP

To use this spell, the caster must be wearing a Green-Haired Wig. In conjunction with this wig, the spell will allow the caster to understand the language of, and communicate with, creatures speaking a non-human tongue (e.g. Goblins, Orcs, etc.).

Cost 1 STAMINA point

YAP

This spell allows the caster to understand the languages of, and communicate with, most animals. It will be ineffective unless the caster is wearing a Green-Haired Wig.

Cost 1 STAMINA point

ZIP

An invaluable aid in close battle, this spell is only usable when the caster is wearing a Ring of Green Metal, such metal having been mined from the Craggen Rock. When the spell is cast on to his ring, it enables the wearer to disappear, and reappear a short distance away. The transportation can be through some soft materials such as wood and clay, but is blocked by stone, metal and the like. It is a rather unreliable spell, though – occasionally it has disastrous results.

Cost 1 STAMINA point

FAR

In conjunction with an Orb of Crystal, this spell will enable its caster to see, with certain limitations, into the future. The Orb must be held in the hands and the spell is recited while concentrating on the Orb. Very little control can be exercised on exactly what will be seen, but the normal tendency is to see near-future events.

Cost 1 STAMINA point

RES

When cast upon a dead human or humanoid creature (i.e. one with two arms, two legs, a head, etc.) while Holy Water is being sprinkled on the corpse, this spell brings it back to life. The resurrection takes some time to work – the body does not simply spring back on its feet – and the ex-corpse can be killed again as normal. For some time after this spell has taken effect, the resurrected creature is dull and dozy, but it may answer questions asked of it by the caster.

Cost 1 STAMINA point

ZED

Casting this spell is beyond the means of most minor conjurers because of the great powers of concentration necessary. In fact, in all known history, this spell has been cast only once. Its caster, a powerful Necromancer from Throben, was never seen again and thus its effects are unknown. The Necromancer's notes were subsequently found, but only indications as to its effects could be assumed. Suffice it to say that this is perhaps *the* most formidable spell in known magic lore – but no living magician knows its true effect.

Cost 7 STAMINA points

Also in Puffins

Steve Jackson's

SORCERY! 1
The Shamutanti Hills

Your search for the legendary Crown of Kings takes you to the Shamutanti Hills. Alive with evil creatures, lawless wanderers and bloodthirsty monsters, the land is riddled with tricks and traps waiting for the unwary traveller. Will you be able to cross the hills safely and proceed to the second part of the adventure – or will you perish in the attempt?

SORCERY! 2
Kharé – Cityport of Traps

As a warrior relying on force of arms, or a wizard trained in magic, you must brave the terror of a city built to trap the unwary. You will need all your wits about you to survive the unimaginable horrors ahead and to make sense of the clues which may lead to your success – or to your doom!

SORCERY! 4
The Crown of Kings

At the end of your long trek, you face the unknown terrors of the Mampang Fortress. Hidden inside the keep is the Crown of Kings – the ultimate goal of the *Sorcery!* epic. But beware! For if you have not defeated the Seven Serpents, your arrival has been anticipated . . .

Complete with all the magical spells you will need, each book can be played either on its own, or as part of the whole epic.

*   *   *   *

Also by Steve Jackson

FIGHTING FANTASY
The introductory Role-playing game

The world of Fighting Fantasy, peopled by Orcs, dragons, zombies and vampires, has captured the imagination of millions of readers world-wide. Thrilling adventures of sword and sorcery come to life in the Fighting Fantasy Gamebooks, where the reader is the hero, dicing with death and demons in search of villains, treasure or freedom.

Now YOU can create your own Fighting Fantasy adventures and send your friends off on dangerous missions! In this clearly written handbook, there are hints on devising combats, monsters to use, tricks and tactics, as well as two mini-adventures complete with GamesMaster's notes for you to start with. Literally countless adventures await you!

WHAT IS DUNGEONS AND DRAGONS?
John Butterfield, Philip Parker, David Honigman

A fascinating guide to the greatest of all role-playing games: it includes detailed background notes, hints on play and dungeon design, strategy and tactics, and will prove invaluable for players and beginners alike.

4.   STARSHIP TRAVELLER
Steve Jackson

Sucked through the appalling nightmare of the Seltsian Void, the starship Traveller emerges at the other side of the black hole into an unknown universe. YOU are the captain of the Traveller and her fate lies in your hands. Will you be able to discover the way back to Earth from the alien peoples and planets you encounter, or will you and your crew be doomed to roam uncharted space forever?

5.   CITY OF THIEVES
Ian Livingstone

Terror stalks the night as Zanbar Bone and his bloodthirsty Moon Dogs hold the prosperous town of Silverton to ransom. YOU are an adventurer, and the merchants of Silverton turn to you in their hour of need. Your mission takes you along dark, twisting streets where thieves, vagabonds and creatures of the night lie in wait to trap the unwary traveller. And beyond lies the most fearsome adventure of them all – the tower stronghold of the infamous Zanbar Bone.

6.   DEATHTRAP DUNGEON
Ian Livingstone

Down in the twisting labyrinth of Fang, unknown horrors await you. Countless adventurers before you have taken up the challenge of the Trial of Champions, but not one has survived. Devised by the devilish mind of Baron Sukumvit, the labyrinth is riddled with fiendish traps and hideous creatures of darkness to trick and test you almost beyond the limits of endurance.

7. ISLAND OF THE LIZARD KING

Ian Livingstone

Kidnapped by a vicious race of Lizard Men from Fire Island, the young men of Oyster Bay face a grim future of slavery, starvation and a lingering death. Their master will be the mad and dangerous Lizard King, who holds sway over his land of mutants by the strange powers of black magic and voodoo. Will you risk all in an attempt to save the prisoners?

Steve Jackson and Ian Livingstone present:

8. SCORPION SWAMP

You're no fool. All your life you've heard tales of Scorpion Swamp and how it is criss-crossed with treacherous paths leading to the haunts of its disgusting denizens. One step out of place spells a certain and lingering death. But now, the swamp holds out the lure of treasure and glory – and you cannot resist the challenge!

9. CAVERNS OF THE SNOW WITCH

Ian Livingstone

Deep within the Crystal Caves of Icefinger Mountains, the dreaded Snow Witch is plotting to bring on a new ice age. A brave trapper dies in your arms and lays the burden of his mission on your shoulders. But time is running out – will You take up the challenge?